Never Come to Rest

by
Keira Michelle Telford

www.venaticpress.com

*"**Audax ad omnia femina,
quae vel amat vel odit.**"*

A woman, when inflamed by love or by hatred,
will dare everything.

CHAPTER

Tuesday June 3, 1913

"WHICH ONE TAKES YOUR FANCY, MILADY?"

The patient shop girl receives no answer.

"The green in this one does complement your eyes ever so nice." She fusses with the colored plumage decorating a lady's straw summer hat, the base of the dyed feathers nestled in an elaborate ruffle of tulle, the whole hat encircled with satin ribbon. "Is it for the races tomorrow? You'll be the most elegant woman at the Derby, I'm sure."

Lady Vera Mae Darlington, the unenthusiastic target of the poor girl's sincere sales patter, stands silently in front of a mirror, gazing at her reflection.

She barely recognizes herself. Glassy emerald eyes stare back at her, devoid of expression, dark circles beneath. They remind her of a china doll she played with as a child: dull and lifeless, liable to shatter at the slightest touch. Her cheeks used to have a natural rosy glow, but no more. Though flawless, her pasty skin has been sapped of its former radiance. Youth is still on her side, but even that, she fears, is fading much too fast.

"You pick." She eases an ostentatiously prettified blue summer hat off her head, careful not to displace a single, tightly pinned lock of dark auburn hair. "It's of little consequence to me either way."

She turns from the mirror, hands over the expensive millinery, and fixes her everyday outing hat back in place, two well-placed hairpins keeping the simple white affair sufficiently secure.

She's had enough. She finds shopping to be a wearisome experience, but at least this excursion has been a momentary diversion from the unparalleled monotony of her daily life, her free time most often spent reading, sewing, or moping—the latter of which she's lately become something of an expert in.

Leaving the shop girl to package up the green hat and a pair of matching gloves—the amount for both added to her account, to be billed at the end of the month—Vera Mae wanders out onto Kensington High Street. It's usually quiet at this time of day, when afternoon is turning into early evening and the shops are about to close, but tonight she spies a gathering of exuberant young women standing outside the imposing Royal Palace Hotel's Empress Rooms.

They're dressed in virginal white from head to toe, their plain outfits ornamented with sashes and armbands in purple, white, and green. Vera Mae recognizes the colors: purple symbolizing dignity, green representing hope for the future, and white for purity. They're the colors of the Women's Social and Political Union, and these women are suffragettes: fierce campaigners for women's rights. Some are wielding large banners, inviting passersby to step inside and peruse the bazaar at their latest fundraising event: All In a Garden Fair, the Suffragette Summer Festival, running from June 3 till June 13. Come and see!

Vera Mae knows she ought not to stray. No good ever comes of a woman exercising her mind, as the man who would call himself her husband is prone to saying, often while reading the latest abominable copy of *The Anti-Suffrage Review*. Yet she yearns for more.

As the shop girl brings out her boxed-up purchases and passes them off to the chauffeur waiting at the curb next to her private motorcar, Vera Mae takes a bold step and seizes the moment. She straightens her plum-colored jacket, grabs a fistful of her ankle-length brocade skirt, hitches it up, and marches into the street.

"Wait here," she directs the disconcerted chauffeur. "I shan't be long."

She strides toward the Empress Rooms while she still has the nerve to do so, and is swiftly funneled into a grand hall hired for the occasion.

It's decorated like a rose garden under an Italian summer sky. White pergolas line the walls, rambling pink roses wound around their columns and woven through their trestles. Beneath these, stalls are set up to sell WSPU merchandise and various other goods donated by the suffragettes to raise money for their cause, the main slogans of which are promoted all around, impossible to ignore.

Votes for women!

Deeds, not words!

At the center of the room, an illuminated fountain draws focus. It's surrounded by a neat grass lawn bedecked with garden chairs, the verdant display edged with box trees painstakingly clipped into intricate shapes. Tucked into the back of the hall, the Ladies' Aeolian Orchestra fills the room with soft, inspiring music.

Another prominent feature of the fair is an impressive plaster statue of Joan of Arc: a symbolic heroine adopted by the suffragettes since her beatification in 1909. The last words she spoke before her execution are inscribed upon the statue's pedestal, and as Vera Mae stops to admire the centerpiece, a tall redhead wearing suffragette colors stands before it in salute and reads the inscription aloud, as if repeating a pledge of allegiance.

"Fight on, and God will give the victory."

"Do you really think so?" Vera Mae wonders, half to herself, half to the redhead. "Do you really think we'll get the vote?"

"Of course!" The redhead beams. "Never doubt it! Justice will prevail! And tomorrow, we shall march one step closer!"

Vera Mae is interested to know what the WSPU could possibly hope to accomplish by holding a suffrage protest on Derby day, when the King and most of London will be at Epsom Downs Racecourse watching the horses run, but the energized redhead doesn't tarry. She hails one of her suffragette comrades and hurries off into the crowds without offering a single word of explanation.

In the wake of her departure, Vera Mae spies a beguiling young woman of near faultless proportions standing beside the fountain.

She's tall and beautiful. Effortlessly beautiful. No more than twenty-five years of age. No need for any powder, lip color, or rouge. Her face is soft and gentle. Perfect cheekbones. Perfect lips. Eyes the color of speedwell. She'd be the absolute embodiment of femininity were it not for the fact that she's wearing a man's suit tailored to fit a woman's form.

There's not a frill on her. Not a single scrap of lace. Black leather ankle boots with a modest heel peek out from the bottom of her gray trousers, the hips and waist of which have been adjusted to accommodate her distinctly womanly curves.

Her matching jacket is open, revealing a single-breasted waistcoat buttoned over a crisp white shirt topped with a silk puff tie. The waistcoat clings snugly to her slender waist and modest bosom, accentuating the evidence of her sex. She wears no gloves. No hat. Her long blonde mane is pulled into a haphazard up-do, locks of honey-colored hair tumbling free.

Other women cluster around her, vying for her attention. One suffragette in particular hangs onto her like seaweed clinging to a rock, leaning tight against her, whispering to her, making her laugh.

The intimacy in their touch is plain to see. Vera Mae watches the statuesque stranger place a hand on the suffragette's lower back, caressing her there, and a sympathetic shiver runs up her spine. Oh, to be touched so daringly! So tenderly! So erotically! Caught staring, she looks away ... briefly. Peeping back seconds later, her gaze is snared by the stranger. Their eyes meet and a smile passes between them.

Feeling a blush color her cheeks, Vera Mae turns her head, cutting the stranger out of her line of sight. Self-conscious, she waits for the heat to subside before she dares to look again, but by the time she does ... the alluring stranger is gone.

Disappointed, she diverts her attention to the stall of suffragette merchandise in front of her. Every inch of the table is cluttered with a muddled array of pamphlets, postcards, flags, scarves, ribbons, and brooches—all in bold WSPU colors. It's an assault to the eyes.

"First time?" A sultry female voice startles her from behind. "You seem overwhelmed."

The alluring, trouser-clad stranger moves in beside her, smiling warmly.

"A little overwhelmed, I suppose." Vera Mae scans the enormous volume of reading material spread over table, suddenly finding herself unable to make eye contact with the object of her fascination. "This isn't really my world." She glances over her shoulder, suffragette colors swarming everywhere. "I'm not sure I quite belong in it."

"You're a woman, yes?" The stranger makes a show of scrutinizing her appearance from top to tail. Especially her tail. "Then I say you belong here just as much as the rest of us."

"Very well." Vera Mae clasps her gloved hands together, suppressing the tremor in them. "So what, may I ask, is the rite of initiation? Must I rush out into the street and set fire to a pillar box?"

The stranger chuckles, but the notion is not entirely implausible. Since the last conciliation bill proposing to grant property-owning women over the age of thirty the right to vote was defeated in the House of Commons in 1912, the determined suffragettes—under the strict control of the WSPU's founder, Emmeline Pankhurst—have resorted to ever more militant tactics. Chaining themselves to railings is no longer protest enough. On an increasingly regular basis, they brazenly commit serious acts of vandalism, including smashing windows and arson. Setting fire to pillar boxes is a particular favorite, along with empty houses and stationary railway carriages. They've even been known to detonate the occasional small bomb. Fortunately, such extreme acts of rebellion are optional.

"The WSPU expects nothing so terribly dramatic." The stranger unpins a 'Votes for Women' brooch from her waistcoat. "Here you are." She fastens the brooch onto Vera Mae's jacket. "Now you're one of us."

"That's all there is to it?" Vera Mae peers down at the adornment.

"Almost." The stranger directs her to a WSPU membership form on the table. "If you want to join the WSPU officially, that'll set you back a shilling, and you'll have to sign a declaration of loyal adherence to the crusade for women's freedom, but the brooch should be enough to inspire you in the right direction."

"How anticlimactic." Vera Mae pulls a face at the form.

"You're disappointed?" The stranger pounces on her apparent dissatisfaction. "Let me guess: you came here hoping for adventure?" She smirks wickedly, her sapphire eyes shimmering. "You wanted something to make your heart pound heavy in your chest."

Vera Mae swallows hard. "My heart is pounding at this moment, I assure you."

"Funny that, so is mine." The stranger captures one of her gloved hands. "May I show you?" She guides Vera Mae's hand to her chest, slips it inside her waistcoat, and lays it over her heart, dangerously close to her breast. "Do you feel it?" She clamps Vera Mae's hand in place. "Do you feel it beating?"

Vera Mae does. It's hammering against her palm, thumping strong and fast ...

Fearing the onset of a faint, she whisks back her hand, keeping her eyes downturned. "So do tell me, what is the most devilish thing you've ever done in the name of your cause? If it's dreadfully wicked, I promise I shan't breathe a word of it to anyone."

"*Our* cause," the stranger corrects her. "We're in this together now, are we not?"

Vera Mae opens her mouth to respond, but the words are lost on her tongue. Another suffragette barges in between them, unapologetically claiming the stranger for herself.

"There you are! I've been looking all over." She helps herself to the stranger's arm. "Are you taking me out for supper, or what? You promised you was gonna be mine tonight. You ain't forgot, have you?"

Awash with a sudden flood of embarrassment, Vera Mae backs away. "I'm sorry." She turns on her heels. "I shouldn't be here."

Before the stranger has a chance to object, she disappears out the door, making a beeline for her waiting motorcar. In her hurry to remove herself from the fair— and from the charming stranger's presence—she forgets to take off the suffrage brooch, and is still wearing it when she steps into her expansive Regent's Park home thirty minutes later. Of course, such a trinket doesn't go unnoticed for long. Within seconds of greeting curmudgeonly Lord Darlington in the library, it becomes an unwelcome focus of the conversation.

"What in God's name is that?" He glowers at the offending piece of jewelry. "You haven't been turned by those militant bitches, have you?"

Vera Mae bites her tongue. "It's nothing, Reginald. Just a silly thing." She removes the brooch, banishing it from view. "Those women cornered me as I was leaving the milliner's."

"Bloody pests," Reginald grumbles. "Ought to be shot."

11

"Yes, indeed." Vera Mae clasps the brooch in her palm. "I'm afraid I've returned rather late. I shall go up and change for dinner at once."

She's glad to excuse herself from the room. The forty-five-year-old, rotund, balding man is in his decline, there's no doubt about that. He's some fifteen years her senior, has a chronic case of gout in his right foot, and his alcohol-reddened cheeks are blemished with tiny broken veins. If he has any redeeming features, she isn't at all sure what they are. He repulses her.

Once safely in her bedroom, alone until her maid arrives to dress her, she opens her palm and admires the brooch, finding a few simple words handwritten in blue ink on the reverse:

Liberty.

No surrender.

CHAPTER

Wednesday June 4, 1913

VERA MAE TRAIPSES ALONG SEVERAL PACES BEHIND Reginald and his doddery aunt, the aging Dowager Baroness, as they wander around the paddock at Epsom Downs Racecourse. Every few moments, they stop to admire one horse or another, praising the proud beast's form and commenting on the odds, hoping for a chance to meet King George as he poses nearby with his horse, Anmer. She has nothing of any value to add.

It's Derby day, and at Reginald's request, she's made extra effort with her appearance. Her shimmering, freshly washed hair is delicately curled, braided, and pinned, her new green hat perched atop the elaborate do. A little powder on her face hides the dark circles beneath her eyes, and her cheeks are glowing and pinkened. Not because she's wearing any rouge, but because the summer heat is stifling inside her high-collared blouse and bengaline jacket.

She ought to have worn a summer dress perhaps, but this outfit is one of her favorites. The five-gore bengaline skirt of silk and wool blend enhances her shapely figure with its vertical stripes of black, olive, and burgundy. The design is simple but flattering. A wide black velvet waistband dips to a V-shaped point at the center front, giving the illusion of a narrower waist and slender hips, and it holds its shape well, making it appear as though she glides smoothly along the ground by some force of divine magic.

Layers of cotton and silk are concealed beneath. In the midday heat, her back is unpleasantly damp, sweat trickling down her spine and soaking into the protective cotton chemise she wears under her corset for just that purpose. She's uncomfortably hot. If she could, she would unfasten the high lace collar of her richly embroidered blouse and fan her upper chest, glad for any small modicum of relief. But she can't. It would be unspeakably improper.

Completing her outfit is a matching bengaline jacket with black pleated lapels and a Chinese braid trim. Darts in the front and back tailor it to fit her figure most precisely, and it clings so snugly to her shoulders that she can't even raise her arms above her head. Not that she would dare to do so at this moment. She's certain her armpits are wet.

Desperate to feel even the faintest whisper of air against her skin, she hooks a finger of one gloved hand over the collar of her blouse and pries it away from her neck, as though loosening the grip of a noose. It doesn't much help.

"Are you sure you're feeling quite up to this, milady?" Bennett, her doting lady's maid, hovers next to her. "If you isn't, you should tell His Lordship. Wouldn't nobody blame you. This is your first big social engagement since ..." She lets that sentence die. "Well, since last year."

"His Lordship has given me little choice in the matter." Vera Mae flinches as a group of boisterous youths barge past her, grazing her person.

Even though she's in a wide open space, she feels confined. People are packed together like sardines, one class brushing shoulders with another, any form of social etiquette markedly absent, children running feral, playing, laughing, and shrieking.

"I must get some air." Vera Mae heads away from the paddock, her anxiety on the rise.

In need of refreshment, she strolls into the adjoining fair in search of a drink. Anything will do, but the stronger the better. With blinkered determination, she passes conjuring acts, clowns, fire breathers, and pugilists, music blaring from all angles, every amusement decorated in gaudy fairground colors. To her left, a steam-driven carousel spins endlessly, the painted horses bobbing up and down, entertaining hordes of squealing youngsters, their fingers sticky with spun sugar. Beside that, a Chair-O-Plane ride starts up, one young woman losing her unsecured straw hat to the wind almost immediately, her pristine up-do soon collapsing into a tangle of flopping, flailing curls.

Not a moment later, the sharp ding of a high striker machine precedes the exultant roar of a crowd of onlookers as a moderately inebriated duke succeeds in testing his strength with the oversized mallet, thus proving his masculinity to the excessively proud woman cheering him on from the sidelines.

Caught off-guard by the sudden burst of noise, Vera Mae takes a sharp draw of breath and comes to an abrupt halt, waiting for her nerves to settle. The frenetic energy of the place is disorienting. There's so much movement. Nearby, a woman giggles as the man escorting her slaps her rump, making some crude remark about her anatomy. Turning from such boorish behavior, Vera Mae withdraws to the outskirts of the fair, only to come upon sounds of an altogether more unwholesome nature emanating from the back of one of the fairground stalls.

"Oh, you're such a beast." A woman moans through the rustling of her skirts and the rhythmic thumping of colliding human flesh.

"Heaven help me," Vera Mae mutters under her breath, retracing her steps to the main thoroughfare. "Where can a woman get some peace in this godforsaken place?"

Still in search of a drink, she braves the masses once more, soon spotting a familiar face trying her luck at a coconut shy. A prepossessing woman with carelessly up-swept blonde hair. A woman wearing men's clothes. And she's not alone. She's accompanied by the young suffragette who'd so gleefully interrupted their flirtatious exchange in the Empress Rooms.

Not wanting to be seen, Vera Mae ducks behind the projecting frontage of a toffee apple stall and spies on the couple from a distance, watching the handsome stranger hurl wooden balls at the carefully positioned coconuts—doing so at the suffragette's behest, no doubt.

"What's milady looking at?" Bennett's voice spooks her.

"Good grief!" Vera Mae presses a hand to her anxiety-tightened chest and glares at her petite, waif-life maid. "Must you follow me about everywhere like a lost puppy?"

Bennett looks suitably apologetic. "His Lordship said I isn't to let you out of my sight."

"Why ever not?" Vera Mae huffs, affronted. "Am I a child?"

"He's afraid you might have another one of your queer spells." Bennett shuffles her feet on the ground. "He says a woman of your nervous condition oughtn't be left alone here."

"Oh, for God's sake." Vera Mae rolls her eyes. "I am quite capable of fetching myself a drink without collapsing into a pitiful heap upon the ground. I do not need a nanny." She digs in her pockets for a few spare coins. "Here, spend this." She tips a generous mix of silver and copper into Bennett's cupped hands. "Stop fussing on me and enjoy yourself."

She shoos Bennett away, quite forgetting to remain hidden, and by the time she returns her attention to the coconut shy, it's too late. She's been spotted. The stranger takes a step toward her, and in a moment of sheer panic, she makes a weak attempt to disappear. Wishing she could vanish herself with the wave of a wand, just as the conjurers seem to do, she weaves left and right and dips between stalls at random, but only succeeds in getting herself lost.

"Do stop running from me." The unrelenting stranger catches up to her behind a fortune teller's tent. "This is absurd."

Defeated, Vera Mae grinds to a standstill and allows herself to be approached.

"Would you care for a coconut?" The stranger bypasses all awkwardness, triumphantly wielding her prize. "I appear to be rather a dab hand at the game."

"Where is your friend?" Vera Mae glances around, seeing hide nor hair of the suffragette. "Might she not like to claim the spoils of your victory?"

"I daresay she is claiming the spoils of someone else's victory as we speak, and doubtless will entice a dozen more hapless souls to engage in the pursuit before the day is out." The stranger allays her concern. "That being the case, I would far rather give my coconut to someone who might genuinely appreciate the gift."

"And you believe that person is me?" Vera Mae eyes the coconut warily.

"Wholeheartedly." The stranger persists with the offer. "It is surely fate that we should meet again so soon."

"Well, who am I to deny fate?" Vera Mae accepts the husk-encased fruit and rolls it in her hands, pondering its structure. "How does one get inside the thing?"

"With immense difficulty." The stranger smirks. "As is the case with all the very best things in life. Especially beautiful women."

Vera Mae raises an immaculately tweezed eyebrow. "Is that so?"

"Absolutely." The smirk becomes a grin. "Shall I let you in on a secret?" She leans close and whispers in Vera Mae's ear. "The very moment you taste the sweet, ripe fruit she hides within—the moment you lap that first

17

precious drop of dew from her weeping, succulent flesh—you realize she is more than worth every effort. Even if you must chase her halfway around Epsom." She lets her soft lips graze Vera Mae's neck. "Tell me your name."

"Why?" Vera Mae mewls and closes her eyes, her breathing labored, goose bumps pricking her skin where the stranger's hot breath tickles her. "Nothing can come of this."

"Are you sure?"

At the sound of nearing footsteps, Vera Mae opens her eyes and withdraws from the stranger with such clumsy haste that she stumbles over a tent peg, horrified to see Bennett standing within eyeshot.

"Milady ..." Bennett doesn't know where to look. "His Lordship is asking for you."

"Milady?" The stranger frowns, taken aback.

"I'm sorry." Vera Mae winces, mortified to be outed so abruptly. "It's best that I go." She returns the coconut to its rightful owner. "I am not worthy of such a gift either."

Backhanding a few escaping tears from her cheeks, she bucks herself up and walks off with Bennett. Once they're well away from the scene of her indiscretion, the embarrassment ebbing away, her palpitations subsiding, she tries to remedy the strained silence between them.

"What you saw is not what you think it to be, Bennett."

"What do I think it to be, milady?" Bennett feigns ignorance. "I'm sure I didn't see aught."

Thankful for her gracious nature, Vera Mae readily accepts the sham. "Not a word to His Lordship."

"Of course not, milady."

Without further word, they rejoin Reginald and the Dowager Lady Darlington, neither one giving any indication that anything is amiss. And so the day wears on. The race begins and Vera Mae settles into her chair atop one of many raised platforms designed to separate the aristocracy from the rabble. The added height affords them a clear view over the heads of those clamoring for a good spot at the edge of the racetrack, including the sweet-tongued stranger.

Vera Mae watches her stop deliberately in front of the platform, smile up, and blow a kiss. It makes her heart thrum. She ought to ignore the gesture but can't.

"Don't do it, milady," Bennett pleads with her. "Stay in your place."

The plea falls on willfully deaf ears. In defiance of the consequences, seized by a sudden burning need to know the name of the woman who so disarms her, Vera Mae rises from her chair and slinks off virtually unnoticed. Reginald is much too invested in the outcome of the race to be distracted by anything going on around him, and the Dowager has enough difficulty remembering where she herself is half the time, never mind worrying on the whereabouts of her daughter-in-law. And Bennett says no more.

Battling her mounting claustrophobia, Vera Mae pushes her way through the jostling crowds. At the same time, a tall redheaded woman holding a suffragette scarf in her left hand ducks under the guardrail and steps out onto the racetrack. Seconds pass. As the horses barrel around Tattenham Corner, their hooves thundering on the ground, kicking up dirt, the woman reaches up with the scarf ...

No-one can help. She is struck by the King's horse, Anmer. Jockey and colt are sent down, and so is she. Her hat flies off. Like a ragdoll, she tumbles over the grass, her limp, broken body trampled by the horse's hooves.

Only a few feet away, Vera Mae witnesses everything. The jockey and horse recover themselves, but the crushed woman—the woman she remembers standing in front of the statue of Joan of Arc in the Empress Rooms—does not.

People flock onto the racetrack to administer aid, and Vera Mae stands motionless in the tide, frozen in dismay, her heart beating erratically, her airways constricted. As her vision closes in and the world becomes a jumbled blur of color, she sees the stranger rushing toward her, and her legs weaken at the knees.

19

"Who are you?" She sinks into the stranger's outstretched arms and slumps downward, unable to keep herself upright. "I must know who you are. I cannot bear it a moment longer."

Crumpled on the ground in the stranger's lap, teetering on the brink of unconsciousness, she feels something being pressed into her palm and instinctively clenches her gloved hand around it. Then there's Bennett.

"Clear off before His Lordship sees you." Bennett dismisses the stranger. "He won't take kindly to help from your sort."

Vera Mae protests incoherently as she's pulled from the stranger's warmth, her cheek then smooshed against the coarse fabric of Bennett's uniform. She tries to hold onto something—anything—but it all slips away. Then there's nothing.

Vera Mae wakes up with a jolt in her luxuriously decorated bedroom. She's lying on her four-poster bed, fully clothed and draped in a blanket, no recollection of how she got there.

"What happened?" she questions Bennett, who's sitting on a straight-backed chair near the vanity, patiently watching over her.

"His Lordship had me give you a tiny drop of chloral to help with your hysterics." Bennett indicates a small bottle of chloral hydrate on the bedside table. "You've been sleeping like a wee babe ever since."

"He drugged me?!" Vera Mae sits up, outraged. "I was *not* hysterical, I was upset. I'd just witnessed ..." She isn't at all sure. "Whatever did I witness?"

Bennett shrugs. "A mad woman leapt in front of the King's horse, so far as I could tell."

"Good God." Vera Mae clutches her head, a migraine threatening to erupt. "And what of the woman who helped me? Who was she? Did she give her name?"

"No, milady. But she left you this." Bennett pulls a small rectangular trade card from a deep pocket in her uniform. "I pried it from your hand, as I believe, had His Lordship seen as I saw, he would've disposed of it directly." She worries the edges of the card with her thumbs, as if debating whether or not to give it over. "That woman what tended to you ... she is, to my reckoning, of an irregular sort."

"A suffragette?"

Bennett shakes her head. "That isn't quite what I'm meaning, milady." She passes Vera Mae the card. "And I think you may know very well what it is I'm meaning." She hesitates to go on. "If I might be permitted to say so, you'd do best to burn that card and refrain from acting upon whatever thoughts you might be having."

Her mood noticeably soured by such frank commentary, Vera Mae shuts down. "Leave me, Bennett." She turns her back to the overstepping maid and pulls the blanket up to her shoulders. "I wish to be alone."

Bennett obeys.

Lying there in silence, Vera Mae peruses the few meager details on the card, gleaning from it that her enthralling stranger is named Eulalie Sauvage, and she's an artist who paints portraits by commission. At the bottom, there's an address and telephone number.

CHAPTER

Thursday June 5, 1913

VERA MAE LOUNGES IN HER BED, TUCKED IN HER SILK sheets, snug beneath the counterpane. She can't bring herself to get up. She hasn't slept. Every time she closes her eyes, she sees the impact of the tall redheaded woman with the King's horse.

Twisted limbs.

Blood.

The snap of bone.

Right on schedule, Bennett arrives to wake her and flings open the room's heavy velvet curtains, welcoming in a fresh summer morning and a stunning view of Regent's Park.

"Rise n'shine, milady." She beams a crooked smile. "Another fine day, so it is."

Finding the lathy brunette's enthusiasm thoroughly nauseating, Vera Mae groans, rolls away from the window, and tucks herself into a fetal ball. "Leave me be," she grumbles, her words muffled by her goose down pillow. "I haven't the energy."

"Come on now. Don't be like that, milady." Bennett adopts an appeasing tone and steps up to the bed, trying to engage her reluctant mistress. "His Lordship wishes for you to take breakfast with him this morning. He was awful insistent about it."

Vera Mae snorts derisively, making no effort to rise.

"Very well, then." Bennett lingers at the bedside, wringing her work-hardened hands. "What apology am I to deliver, milady? Shall I say that you're unwell again?" She chews on her chapped lower lip. "He gets ever so cross with me when I tells him that."

Vera Mae half opens one eye and peers up at her anxious, fidgeting maid through long, beeswax-coated eyelashes. She ought not to keep sending the poor timid girl to suffer the brunt of His Crotchety Lordship's escalating frustrations. The beast must be appeased on occasion, and she must be the one to do it.

With an exaggerated sigh of resignation, she throws the quilted counterpane off her nightgown-clad body, heaves herself upright, and swings her legs out of bed. In a flash, Bennett is kneeling at her feet with a basin of warm water, a flake of soap, a washcloth, and a towel.

"You're being a jolly good sport, milady." Bennett works a soapy lather up on her hands and washes Vera Mae's dainty feet, taking extra care between her toes. "His Lordship's mood is ever so much improved when you show him a kindness."

Once each foot is perfectly clean and dry, her nails buffed up to a pearly sheen, Vera Mae crosses the room to the washstand and conducts the rest of her morning ablutions before sitting at the vanity, loath to confront her wan reflection in the mirror.

"P'raps you'd like a little dab of rouge on them snowy cheeks today, milady?" Bennett attempts to cheer her. "No more than a light dusting of course."

"Why pretend?" Vera Mae gazes at her pale, dry lips, lamenting how long it's been since she was last kissed. "Who is it that I must impress with my healthy pallor and vitality?"

Bennett offers no answer for that. In silence, she unravels Vera Mae's long auburn hair from a loose braid and brushes it out, parting it at the side before sweeping it all back and pinning it in a decorative low bun above the nape of her neck. To finish, she eases in some pearl-tipped hair pins, nestling them so deeply into the various loops and twists of the up-do that only the shiny ornamental pearls remain visible.

"There you are, milady." She makes sure every last strand of hair is tucked into place, then retrieves today's preselected morning outfit from the dressing room, along with an armful of undergarments: chemise, satin directoire knickers, corset, stockings, camisole, and petticoat.

The routine never deviates. Vera Mae whisks off her nightgown and stands in front of a cheval mirror, waiting to be dressed, her nude body on display for the briefest of moments before being covered by the cap-sleeved plain cotton chemise. She has others that are much more elaborate in design. Some are silk and lace, meant to titillate more than they are to preserve one's modesty, but she seldom wears them. What would be the point? There's no-one to titillate.

Next, the knee-length, wide-legged knickers, and then the corset. Bennett cinches her into the restrictive garment from bust to hips, tightening the laces as much as she can from Vera Mae's waist downward, slenderizing every curve except her full, proud bosom.

Skin never touches skin. Bennett rolls on Vera Mae's cotton day stockings and fixes them to the garter straps attached to the corset without so much as grazing her smooth legs, then has her step into an ankle-length silk petticoat and fastens it in place around her waist.

"There aren't enough hours in the day for all this nonsense," Vera Mae gripes.

"Almost done, milady." Bennett helps her into a button-up camisole to wear over her corset, then urges her into a tailored, high-collared blouse, gored skirt, and a pair of spotlessly polished ankle boots.

At the finish of the exhaustive enterprise—a rigmarole which could be repeated four or five times throughout the day, depending on her choice of social and leisure activities—Vera Mae is covered from neck to toe. A little jewelry is added for ornament—earrings, bracelets, and the like—and she makes her way downstairs to the breakfast room. Therein, she finds Reginald in a typical state of disgruntlement, something in one of the morning papers having set him on a tirade against the women's suffrage movement.

"The whole bloody lot of them ought to be locked up. Can't be trusted to behave rationally, and they want the vote! Ha! Insubordinate wretches." He condemns the tirelessly crusading suffragettes without looking up from his crisp, recently ironed newspaper. "Abominable conduct, that's what it is. The whole day was ruined by some lunatic woman. And do you know what Her Ladyship did?" He directs his question to the stoic, gray-haired butler standing by at the periphery of the room. "The damned fool nearly threw herself on the racecourse in sympathy." He slaps the newspaper onto the breakfast table, only then noticing that Vera Mae has entered the room.

"Good morning, Reginald." Vera Mae takes the seat opposite him at the small round table and peeks at the headline news, not daring to reach out and take the paper from him lest she should be accused of harboring an unhealthy curiosity for the cause.

"Good morning, my dearest." He greets her with an exaggerated level of enthusiasm, his arms outstretched as though he's witnessing a divine miracle. "How magnanimous of you to grace me with your presence."

Vera Mae halts in the midst of unraveling her napkin. "Consider this fair warning: if you have the audacity to say even so much as one more sarcastic word to me, I shall go straight back up to bed and you will not see me for a week."

Laughing, Reginald extends a fat-fingered hand across the table and clamps it over hers, dwarfing her slender digits beneath it. "I'm glad of your company."

Not even that sounds entirely sincere. Vera Mae forces a weak smile, only managing to hold it on her lips for a second or two before she tires of the pretence and lets it melt away. Indeed, as the months drag on, she's finding it increasingly difficult to look at him without feeling a small measure of revulsion.

Hoping to get through breakfast with minimal conversation, she turns her attention to the feast of fruit, toast, crumpets, bacon, and omelets laid out in front of her. It's more food than two people could ever possibly consume in one sitting, and she has little appetite for any of it. Still, not wanting to be rude, she plucks a triangular slice of cold toast from the rack, slathers butter on it, and nibbles at the corner.

"How are you feeling this morning?" Reginald helps himself to another rasher of bacon, having probably devoured most of the pig already. "After all that nasty business at Epsom."

"A little out of sorts, but I shall recover."

He doesn't seem to care. "What I can't fathom is what on Earth you thought you were doing darting out into the fray like that." He swills the bacon down with a gulp of whiskey. "What possible assistance could you have offered that idiot woman?"

Vera Mae bites back a venomous response. "It was instinct." She thinks of Eulalie Sauvage. "I saw her and felt compelled to go to her."

Reginald guffaws. "There you are, you see! None of you make any damn sense." He checks the time on his gold pocket watch, preparing to leave. "Perhaps that's what you need, though: to be around your own kind. The company of another woman might prove to be something of a tonic for your doldrums."

"I couldn't agree more." Vera Mae suppresses a smile, keeping her enthusiasm for the venture in tight check lest he should feel encouraged to force her participation in a sewing circle, or some other mundane pursuit deemed suitable for a woman.

"Right, I must be off." Reginald finishes his drink and gets to his feet, straightening his suit. "Try to put a pleasant face on today, won't you? It isn't attractive when you're so morose."

As he leans over to plant a clumsy kiss on the top of her head, Vera Mae is engulfed with a waft of liquor so strong it makes her instantly woozy. On a good day, his breath could take down an ox from fifty feet.

Once alone, she pushes away her breakfast plate, props her elbows on the table, and relaxes as much as her rigid corsetry will allow. Keen to remain abreast of recent events—even if she must keep her opinions about them to herself—she thieves Reginald's abandoned copy of *The Morning Post* and scours it for news about the poor suffragette at Epsom, whose name she learns is Emily Wilding Davison.

The fearless activist is currently in critical condition, fighting for her life in Epsom Cottage Hospital. Doctors have done their best for her, but she remains unconscious and recovery does not seem likely.

"Good Lord." Vera Mae pores over the details. "Other women are out there risking their lives for political equality while I'm doing what? Absolutely nothing of any importance whatsoever." She aims her private commentary toward an apathetic white cat lounging on a velvet cushion near her feet. "I'm about as useless as you are."

Seeming to take offense at that, the ornery feline retorts with a sharp meow and repositions, aiming its derrière in her direction, tail up, privy parts bared.

"Oh, have you no shame at all?" Vera Mae lays her napkin over the lower half of the cat's body, covering it up. "I've told you before: nobody wants to see your vulgar bits and pieces."

Another meow.

Of all the animals presented to her in the last year, Madam Catkins—Reginald's latest well-intentioned but miserably unsuccessful attempt to draw her out of her spiraling melancholia—is her least favorite. Always disgracing herself in polite company, whether by presenting her posterior in the most unladylike manner or by casually licking her unmentionables, Madam

Catkins is not in the least bit cut out for society life. As a result, she joins a string of other fluffy and feathery failures, including the pair of lovebirds now relegated to the billiards room, the albino peacock seen occasionally roaming freely throughout Regent's Park, and the overly chatty guinea pig now happily doted on by the servants below stairs.

Gifts, animal or otherwise, have never yet had any beneficial effect on her mood, but his latest idea ... to cultivate a female friendship ...

Vera Mae pulls Eulalie Sauvage's trade card out of her pocket, where the 'Votes for Women' brooch is also safely secreted. Dare she?

The butler returns presently. "Is there anything I can do for you this morning, milady?"

"You know what? I think there is." She hands him the card. "Telephone this number and arrange for the artist, Miss Sauvage, to come by here at her earliest convenience." Her stomach flips in anticipation. "I wish to have my portrait painted."

CHAPTER

Friday June 6, 1913

VERA MAE TRIES TO RELAX IN THE DRAWING ROOM AFTER luncheon, but her ability to concentrate on anything is severely hampered by her nerves. She keeps glancing at the ticking clock on the mantel, impatiently awaiting the arrival of Eulalie Sauvage.

Now in her second outfit of the day—a flowing light blue afternoon dress accessorized with matching satin gloves—she's also longing for the coming of five o'clock, when it will, for a few short hours before dinner, become acceptable to release herself from the confines of her corset and lounge about the house in her tea gown. Thank goodness for small pleasures.

In need of something to occupy her mind, she attempts to read, flicking through the pages of a book with little interest, not caring anything for the chaste romance played out in the text. She tried the newspaper earlier, but didn't care much for the news therein. Yesterday, Muswell Hill cricket pavilion became the latest target of the suffragettes' campaign of arson.

"Pardon the disruption, milady." The butler appears in the open doorway, standing tall in his starched livery. "The artist you requested is here to see you." He hesitates to say more. "I've set her up in the library, but I should warn you, she appears to be rather ... peculiar."

By the look on his face, anyone would think he were referring to a woman exhibiting some hideous deformity worthy of an old P. T. Barnum traveling show.

"Peculiar?" Vera Mae abandons her book. "Whatever can you mean?" She feigns ignorance, finding amusement in pressing him on what is evidently an awkward subject.

"She doesn't look quite as one would expect a woman to look." He avoids addressing the nature of her peculiarity in any greater detail. "But you mustn't be shocked by it, milady. These bohemian types so often are a little on the eccentric side of things."

"I shall keep that in mind." Vera Mae walks calmly out of the drawing room, but breaks into a canter as soon as she's out of the butler's sight.

Giddy like a young girl about to attend her first dance, she dashes to the library, taking a moment to gather herself outside the door before striding in with a practiced air of cool indifference—a trademark of her class.

Inside, Eulalie Sauvage is standing at a large stretched canvas propped on an easel in the center of the room, a pencil tucked behind her ear, an array of other drawing implements laid out on a side table beside a small wooden stool. With her jacket cast off over the back of a chair, her upper body is on display, hugged by a fitted single-breasted waistcoat buttoned over a pristine white shirt, the sleeves rolled up to her elbows, baring her lightly sun-kissed skin.

Hearing Vera Mae enter, she turns to greet her host. "Well, well, well." Her lips curl into a broad smile. "I'd hoped my mysterious lady subject might be you."

Today, she wears a length of red satin ribbon in her hair, tied around her head to keep any loose curls of her honey-colored mane from falling in her face as she works.

It's an unexpectedly feminine touch. She looks divine, and while gazing reverently at her, Vera Mae momentarily loses the capacity for speech.

"I'm sorry, milady. I seem to have forgotten all my manners." Eulalie wipes her hands on a paint-stained rag dangling from her trouser pocket and steps forward, filling the silence. "My name is Eulalie Sauvage, as you now know, and it's a great pleasure to formally meet you." She extends an ungloved hand, unwittingly violating an unspoken set of deeply ingrained social customs by failing to wait for Vera Mae to initiate the introduction.

"I trust that you are well rested after the calamity at Epsom?" she continues. "I've had women fall for me before, but I must say, you're the first who's ever done so literally."

Vera Mae's jaw slackens. Her mouth moves, but no sound comes out.

"Forgive me." Eulalie withdraws slightly. "I've been bold with you. Much too bold. I fear I've displeased you."

"No, not a bit." Vera Mae recovers her wits and reaches for Eulalie's proffered hand before the opportunity expires. "Your unruly tongue took me by surprise, that's all. No-one's ever dared to speak to me so plainly." She rectifies the situation with a light handshake. "It's a delight to have you here. Truly it is."

"I'm glad." Eulalie keeps hold of Vera Mae's satin-encased hand, bends slightly at the waist, and dips forward, pressing a soft kiss to her knuckles. "We're going to be spending a considerable amount of time together over the coming days, and I should hate to think that I'd made myself unwelcome already."

"Certainly not," Vera Mae assures her. "I'm looking forward to it." Her fingers tingle where Eulalie's lips touched. "As are you, I trust."

"Nothing will give me greater pleasure." Eulalie straightens up but doesn't let go, her bright blue eyes locked on Vera Mae's subdued greens.

A second passes.

Shying from the intensity, Vera Mae averts her gaze. "You have the most unusual name, yet it sounds familiar to me." She cocks her head, delving through her memory banks for any smidgen of recollection. "Eulalie ... where have I heard it before?"

"Have you read much of Edgar Allan Poe?" Eulalie finally lets their hands slip away from each other. "It's taken from a poem of his."

"Not a terribly morbid one, I hope." Vera Mae mourns the loss of contact.

"Far from it." Eulalie presses a hand over her heart. "It's about love. A deep, ardent love."

Blushing furiously, Vera Mae changes the subject. "Do you always dress this way?" She trails her eyes freely up and down Eulalie's body. "You're very unique."

"Most say peculiar." Eulalie chuckles. "There's no need to be careful with my feelings, milady. I know what people think of me."

"I get the distinct impression that you're not the sort of woman who gives two figs what others think of her, and I respect that a great deal." Vera Mae's mind drifts back to Epsom Downs Racecourse and Emily Wilding Davison. "The world needs more brave women."

"Any woman can be brave if she wants to be." Eulalie flashes her an encouraging smile. "When her passions are suitably inflamed, a woman is capable of anything."

"Perhaps." Vera Mae sighs, wishing she'd had the courage to make different life choices. "Sadly, passion can be a very dangerous thing for a woman in my position." She invites Eulalie to sit. "Shall we begin? How do you want me?"

"However you please." Eulalie retreats to her easel. "Your husband left no particular instruction, except to say that I ought to make you beautiful. But doing so will be no great difficulty for me, since I believe you are the most exquisite specimen of womanhood I've ever had the good fortune to cast my eyes upon."

That coaxes a small smile from Vera Mae's lips. "You flatter me shamelessly." She opts for the sofa beside the fireplace, easing herself into it with her rump projected outward and her torso completely straight, her range of movement severely inhibited by the inflexibility of her undergarments. "But you are mistaken about one critical thing: the man who telephoned you on my behalf is most definitely not my husband. He is the butler."

"I do beg your pardon, milady." Eulalie positions her easel for the best view of her subject. "I assumed I was speaking with the gentleman who accompanied you to the Derby."

"He is not my husband, either." Disgust seeps into Vera Mae's voice. "He intends to make a wife of me, but has not yet succeeded in the endeavor."

"Yet?" Eulalie arches an eyebrow. "So there is hope for him?"

Vera Mae dips her head, as if she might find the answer to that on the floor by her feet. "It's very complicated," she says at last, smoothing out the creases in her dress, in need of something to keep her hands busy.

"But you are not enamored with the prospect of holy matrimony." Eulalie touches pencil to canvas, beginning to outline the work. "You do not love him."

"What business is that of yours?" Vera Mae scowls, affronted by the audacity of her presumption. "The man has his faults, certainly, but I believe he truly does care for me in some way."

"And that is enough for you?" Eulalie steps onto thin ice.

"How dare you ask me such a thing." Vera Mae glares indignantly at her. "I must be grateful to him. He has gone to great lengths trying to raise my spirits these past few months, and I've not made it easy. My zest has been chronically depleted of late."

"Why?" Eulalie plods on. "Have you been unwell?"

"No, widowed."

A heavy silence descends upon the room.

"I'm sorry." Eulalie lifts her pencil from the canvas. "It isn't my place to ask you these things, and you have every right to be cross with me, but I ..." She sighs. "I hate seeing a woman fall into marriage for the wrong reasons.

It happens all too often, and I know what it does to a woman's soul." She slouches forward, resting her elbows on her knees. "Please, I beg of you, do not marry this man because you feel you owe him a debt. It will crush you."

A tear cascades down Vera Mae's cheek. "I know." She retrieves a hanky from her pocket and dabs away her sorrow. "My entire life has been spent pleasing anyone and everyone except myself."

"Until the day you walked into a suffragette fair in Kensington." Eulalie cracks a smile.

"Indeed." Vera Mae attempts a weak laugh. "His Lordship would have a fit if he knew where I'd been." She sniffles. "He goes to all those haughty gentlemen's clubs in Pall Mall, and he's a member of the National League for Opposing Woman Suffrage. In fact, he's on the damn executive committee. Do you know who they are? They produce that rotten magazine, *The Anti-Suffrage Review*. Have you ever read such nonsense? They believe giving us women the vote will have a deteriorating influence on our character."

Eulalie abandons her post at the easel and joins Vera Mae on the sofa. "Now you're talking like a proper suffragette."

"And you're encouraging me." Vera Mae smiles through her tears. "May I confess something to you?"

"Of course." Eulalie shuffles closer. "What is it?"

"When my husband died last year, a part of me felt relieved. Is that terribly wicked of me?" Vera Mae blows her nose on the sodden hanky. "I was released from my marital obligations, and it felt as though a great weight had been lifted from my shoulders." Teardrops cling to her eyelashes, breaking free and tumbling down her face when she blinks. "I do not believe I've ever truly cried for the man in grief, only guilt. I'm such a dreadful woman."

"Never think that." Eulalie reaches out to her. "We cannot help what we feel, nor who we feel it for." She hesitates. "If you don't mind my asking, what happened to your husband? You're so young to be made a widow."

"It was an accident." Vera Mae chokes back tears. "He wished to embark upon some new business venture in New York City, but never made it there. The ship he was aboard sank in the north Atlantic Ocean after it struck an iceberg. They never recovered his body."

"Oh, my God ... the RMS Titanic." Eulalie lays a hand on her knee. "Were you with him?"

"I was fortunate. Many others were not." Vera Mae stiffens at her touch. "There are no words to describe the horror of that night. Even now, when I'm alone in a crowd of people, I feel these pains in my chest and I cannot breathe. I need space. I need air. I need ..." Her words trail off. "Do ignore me. I'm such a frightful mess."

Eulalie squeezes her knee. "It's perfectly understandable."

At the brush of her fingertips, Vera Mae scoots out of her reach. "You should leave now. I'm very tired." She backs against the arm of the sofa, completely extricating herself from the risk of further physical contact. "May we continue this portrait another day?"

"Absolutely." Eulalie draws away from her. "Anything you wish."

Without further word or protest, Eulalie collects her smaller painting supplies, taking anything that will fit inside her leather satchel. She leaves behind the easel and the canvas, and a few other non-essential items, scoops up her jacket, and heads for the door. She isn't even out of the room before Vera Mae collapses in hysterics on the sofa, sobbing into the velvet cushions, her shoulders heaving with each muffled wail.

CHAPTER

Saturday June 7, 1913

VERA MAE STANDS IN THE LIBRARY, SCRUTINIZING THE pencil-drawn beginnings of her portrait, seeing the outline of a demure woman with thin lips and a somber expression, sadness in her vacant eyes. There's beauty in her too, but it's masked by a heavy sorrow.

She hears Reginald enter the room behind her, but doesn't turn to greet him. Having taken her breakfast in bed yet again, as is her prerogative, she knows he'll be displeased.

"I missed you this morning, darling." He invades her personal space and pecks her cheek. "I do wish you'd be more generous with your time."

She says nothing.

"What's going on here?" He frowns at the canvas, the artwork too incomplete to properly assess. "You're having your portrait painted? Whatever for?"

"Do I need a reason?"

Reginald shrugs. "You haven't mentioned it."

"It was all rather spur of the moment." Vera Mae offers no apology. "In any case, I wasn't aware that I needed your permission."

Reginald bends to inspect the portrait at closer range. "The man must be jolly good. He's captured the misery of you." He bumps his leg against Eulalie's stool, knocking something hard onto the floor. "Is that a damned coconut?" He picks it up.

Oblivious to its presence until then, Vera Mae snatches it from him. "It's *my* coconut." She holds it protectively against her chest. "You cannot have it."

"Why on Earth would I want the revolting thing?" He looks queerly at her, as one might look at a monkey smoking a pipe, or some other exotic animal behaving in a manner quite unlike itself. "You are becoming increasingly odd."

"Better that than a bore." She pushes past him, coconut in hand, and seeks out the tirelessly working butler, barging in on him as he's filling the brandy decanter in the drawing room, causing him to spill a small quantity on the mahogany sideboard.

"I wish to continue with the portrait," she declares emphatically, the coconut gripped securely between her hands and bosom.

"When, milady?" He tries not to look at the coconut.

"Immediately." She beams a rare smile. "Send for Miss Sauvage at once, and find Bennett. I shall be needing a change of clothes."

Vera Mae undresses to her knickers, stockings, and chemise, leaving her clothes in a billowy heap on her bedroom floor before rifling through a selection of outfits laid out on her bed, searching for the perfect gown. Having only recently emerged from the obligatory period of mourning, her wardrobe is in dire need of updating. Much of it is still far too dark and dreary for her liking.

"Is this the one you wanted, milady?" Bennett appears in the doorway holding an extravagant pink satin corset decorated with white lace and a red silk bow at the bust. "You hasn't worn this bit of lingerie for an age."

"Yes, well, I'm wearing it today." Vera Mae snaps her fingers. "Hurry, hurry. She's here already. I don't want to keep her waiting."

"Is this for the artist, milady?" Ever-obedient Bennett begins lacing her into the corset.

"What of it?" Vera Mae responds sharply.

"Nothing, milady." Bennett pulls the laces taut. "It isn't my place to judge."

Vera Mae gasps, the corset cinched too tightly around her waist. "Careful!" She slaps Bennett's hands away. "Allow me to breathe, will you?"

Bennett mumbles an apology, loosens the corset, and helps her into the rest of her clothes without saying another word.

Ten minutes later, Vera Mae breezes into the library wearing a red silk dress, her décolletage exposed, her abundant cleavage on display. Eulalie rises from the stool to greet her, but is rendered speechless by the sight.

"Am I suitably dressed?" Vera Mae prompts her.

"You look absolutely ravishing." Eulalie pins her eyes on Vera Mae's plentiful personal attractions.

Pleased with that response, Vera Mae soaks up the attention, enjoying the novelty of being so brazenly leered at. But it doesn't last. Madam Catkins trots into the room uninvited and steals Eulalie's interest. Not because she's been recently bathed or groomed, but because she's wearing a tiny pair of knitted trousers and a matching bonnet, the latter complete with ear holes and a delicate lace trim.

"Why is your cat wearing trousers?" Eulalie frowns.

"Because she is the most immodest creature I've ever had the misfortune to call a pet." Vera Mae glowers at the unwanted feline. "Always parading about the house with her rear quarters on display. It's obscene."

Eulalie stifles a laugh.

"What's so funny?" Vera Mae crosses the room and seats herself on the sofa, arms folded defensively. "I'm sick to death of looking at her bum-be-doo."

Eulalie struggles to keep a straight face. "And what purpose the bonnet?"

"I had extra yarn."

Unable to contain it, Eulalie's laugh breaks free.

"Oh, go ahead. Mock me as you will." Vera Mae relaxes her arms, conceding the ridiculousness of it. "This is what I've been reduced to."

"I've never met anyone so perturbed by feline anatomy. You need a more productive hobby." Eulalie's laughter ebbs away, her gaze once again snared by Vera Mae. "Before we start, may I pose you?"

Vera Mae doesn't voice an objection to the proposition, so Eulalie plucks a single red rose from a vase on the mantel and coaxes her to remove her gloves so that she might grasp it lightly in her hands, her dress eased off one shoulder, baring more alabaster skin. The rigidity of her undergarments restricts all movement, but Eulalie manages to make her appear comfortable.

"How long will this take?" Vera Mae wonders, fearing the contorted position she's been placed in—propped against the corner of the sofa, half reclined—is likely to become intolerable in an inordinately short amount of time.

"Till you grow weary of my company." Eulalie winks.

"What if you grow weary of mine?"

"Impossible, milady." Eulalie takes her place behind her easel and gets to work, satisfied with the setting of things. "It's a joy merely to look at you."

"There's that sweet tongue of yours again." Vera Mae blushes. "You're really too kind. Especially after I made such a fool of myself yesterday."

"You're no fool to be upset, milady." Eulalie flits her eyes between subject and canvas. "What happened to you was ... unthinkable."

"All the same, I ought to be in better control of myself." Vera Mae rolls the stem of the rose between her fingers, letting the velvety petals graze her glossy, carmine-tinted lips, their natural color enhanced with a little paste. "Let's not speak of it again."

At that, the gloomy matter is dropped and they drift instead from one easy topic to another, their light conversation punctuated by periods of contented silence and the occasional titter, the portrait session continuing until Vera Mae begins to fidget uneasily, incapable of maintaining her statue-like pose any longer.

Responding to her obvious discomfort, Eulalie lays down her brush. "I think a break is in order for us both. Would you like to take a walk with me?"

"A walk?" Vera Mae sits up straight. "Where? Outside?"

"Where else?" Eulalie rises and stretches. "You live on the outskirts of the most delightful park in all of London. Why not make the most of it?"

"All right." Vera Mae struggles to get up from the sofa, her body stiff from holding an unnatural position for so long. "Let me go up and change."

She takes a step, but her foot refuses to bear her weight. Pins and needles shoot through her ankle and calf, radiating up to her knee, and she totters precariously in front of the fireplace, unable to keep her balance. Coming to her rescue, Eulalie seizes one of her flailing hands and steadies her, the gesture met with a whimper of startled gratitude.

The touch of their bare hands is the first direct skin-to-skin contact Vera Mae's had in a painfully long time. Lost for words, she stares at the bridge between their bodies, overwhelmed by the sensation of Eulalie's strong but gentle fingers clasped around her own, all barriers gone.

"What's wrong?" Eulalie seeks to draw her closer, but she rebuffs the advance.

43

"I'll be right back." She tears herself away. "I must be appropriately attired."

Leaving Eulalie looking bewildered by her behavior, she slinks upstairs to change into an outfit more suitable for promenading in the park: a skirt and blouse ensemble accessorized with a decorative satin bowtie, a straw hat boasting far too many feathers, and yet another pair of gloves. When she returns, Eulalie is waiting for her at the front door, one arm crooked for her to take.

"Very well." She accepts, enchanted by Eulalie's devotion to the role. "You may play the part of the gentleman."

Arm in arm, they cross the street to Regent's Park and stroll with no particular aim, discussing this and that, including the suffragette arson attack on the park's refreshments rooms last February. The repair work cost the vast sum of six hundred and fifty pounds, and Reginald was predictably enraged by the whole affair.

"I've never heard him use so much profanity," Vera Mae recalls with amusement. "His face went such a shade of red I thought he might explode at any minute." She stops suddenly beneath the shade of a small copse of trees, her ears pricked for something. "Do you hear that?"

Breaking away from Eulalie, she wanders off the footpath and through the grass, following a frantic high-pitched chirruping to the base of a tree, where she finds a frightened baby bird flapping its immature, stubby wings.

"Oh, look at the poor darling!" She crouches beside it. "He's all alone."

"Too young to be a fledgling," Eulalie surmises, scooping him into her hands. "He must've fallen from his nest." She peers skyward, spotting a muddle of twigs nestled in the fork of two thick branches sprouting from the trunk of the oak.

"He's such an adorable little thing." Vera Mae admires him. "Is he soft? He looks soft."

"Touch him." Eulalie holds the bird out to her. "Take off your gloves."

With some hesitancy, Vera Mae pulls off her kid gloves and brings a hand to the helpless baby, stroking her fingertips along his fluffy plumage. That brings a smile to her at first, but it quickly fades.

"Will he die?"

"Not if I can help it." Eulalie buoys her spirits. "I shall return the unhappy fellow to his nest at once."

Vera Mae dare not ask how, and she doesn't need to. Eulalie answers her unspoken question by tucking the little bird into the chest pocket of her waistcoat and removing her jacket.

"Would you be so kind?" She hands the jacket to Vera Mae and begins to climb the tree.

"Oh, you can't be serious." Vera Mae watches her go up. "For goodness sake! Come down from there at once! You shall fall and cause yourself a terrible injury."

"Then you will have to nurse me back to health." Eulalie continues her ascent undaunted.

"I supposed I should be flattered that you have so much faith in me," Vera Mae calls up to her, anxiously clutching the jacket, inhaling the scent of Eulalie's perfume on the fabric. "But I very much doubt that I am qualified for such an undertaking."

Afraid that Eulalie will lose her footing and break her neck, Vera Mae fights the urge to cover her eyes. Wincing all the while, she waits with bated breath as Eulalie replaces the baby in its nest with its squawking, hungry siblings, and doesn't dare breathe a sigh of relief until she's safely back on the ground.

"You really are very brave." She keeps Eulalie's jacket hugged in her arms. "I do believe I'm in some very real danger of swooning."

"I shall be here to catch you if you do." Eulalie lays her hands on Vera Mae's slender waist. "You know I will."

Palpably affected by Eulalie's proximity, Vera Mae tenses, gripping the jacket so tight her knuckles turn white. "What kind of woman are you?"

"I'm certain you know precisely the kind of woman I am, milady." Eulalie takes a step closer. "And I have a notion that we are not so different from one another in that regard. Am I right?"

Vera Mae has no time to formulate an answer. Without warning, the heavens open. Rain pours down, soaking her blouse and wilting the feathers in her hat. Eulalie helps her into the jacket, but it does little to help, so they throw grace and refinement to the wind and run for the house, holding hands all the way.

CHAPTER

VERA MAE AND EULALIE SPILL IN THROUGH THE FRONT door of the Regent's Park house in fits of uncontrollable laughter, both drenched to the bone, water dripping from their clothes and puddling on the tiled floor around their feet.

Two servants who happen to be in the hall to witness their cacophonous entrance gawk at Vera Mae, shocked to see her so bedraggled—and laughing! Disliking the openly astonished looks on their faces, Vera Mae tries to compose herself.

"We require a change of clothes." She backhands limp, wet hair from her face. "Send Bennett up to my room directly."

As the servants scurry away, Vera Mae leads Eulalie up the grand staircase and into her sumptuously decorated bedroom, the furnishings draped in the finest lace and silk, everything pristine and in its place—including Eulalie's coconut on the bedside table.

"I feel like a drowned rat." She flings her soggy hat onto the vanity and catches a glimpse of her reflection in the mirror. "I suppose I rather look like one as well." She slips off Eulalie's jacket and tosses it onto an ottoman at the foot of the bed. "We really ought to get out of all these wet clothes before we catch our death of cold, don't you think?"

She faces Eulalie and unbuttons her blouse, peeling it away from her glistening skin with a flourish and casting it off onto the ottoman. Following her lead, Eulalie removes her waistcoat and gives it the same treatment. Next, Vera Mae sheds her saturated skirt, letting it collapse in a heap around her ankles. Eulalie responds by doffing her silk puff tie, slipping her suspenders off her shoulders, and undoing her trousers.

Without breaking eye contact, Vera Mae begins working on the buttons of her camisole, revealing her lavish corset inch by inch as Eulalie starts on the buttons of her shirt, the joint unveiling coordinated with perfect synchronicity. After the last button, they whisk off their garments in unison, this simultaneous disrobing leaving Vera Mae in her corset and chemise, and Eulalie in a cotton camisole.

In order to bare her corset completely, Vera Mae eases her petticoat off her hips and sends it the way of her skirt, exposing her stockings and knickers in the process.

"I suppose you disapprove of corsets." She unclips her garters, propping her feet on the ottoman one at a time in order to do so without bending. "Being a modern woman and all, you surely must." She runs both hands from her hips to her waist to her ribcage, then up to her bust, directing Eulalie's gaze over her body.

"Not at this moment." Eulalie ogles her without reservation. "In fact, at this moment, I have to say I'm very much in favor of them."

"Still, I'm certain you'd rather I liberated myself from it." Vera Mae grasps the center busk of the expensive garment, preparing to unfasten it using the front hook and eye clasps designed for speed and ease. "Wouldn't you?" She pops the top clasp.

"Oh, God, yes." Eulalie glues her eyes to Vera Mae's hands. "Please do."

Her breasts aching for release, Vera Mae unhooks the corset slowly, taking her time with each clasp. When she reaches the bottom, she pulls the corset away, her unfettered charms shielded from Eulalie's eyes only by her cotton chemise, her hardened nipples clearly visible.

Ready to reciprocate, Eulalie fumbles with her camisole, keen to tear it off over her head, but Bennett's inopportune arrival disrupts the show.

"Oh, you've got yourself in such a state, milady." Bennett fusses over her mistress. "You're soaked right down to your drawers!" She hands Vera Mae a small towel and fetches some dry clothes from the dressing room, but Vera Mae vetoes the selection as soon as she spots another corset and blouse in her hands.

"No, we shan't bother with all that." She dries off her face, arms, and neck with the towel. "It's almost five o'clock. A tea gown will do."

"Very good, milady." Bennett amends her outfit choice without complaint.

Unable to be quite so overt with her flirtations in Bennett's presence, Vera Mae turns her back to Eulalie for the finale of her denuding. Ensuring that she's standing in Eulalie's sightline, their eyes meeting in the vanity mirror, she begins to lift her chemise, but Bennett sweeps in behind her holding a thick white sheet, using it like a screen to protect her modesty until she's stripped, dried, and clothed in fresh undergarments—sans corset.

That done, Bennett helps her into a pale blue tea gown. "It's good to see you with some color in your cheeks, milady." She buttons up the dress at the back, making sure every frill and ruffle is in place. "You do look ever so happy."

"I have Miss Sauvage to thank for that." Vera Mae tosses her guest the towel. "Do find her something appropriate to wear, won't you? Something from my late husband's wardrobe will be more suited to her tastes than anything from mine."

Bennett hesitates.

"Go on now," Vera Mae insists. "Do as I say."

Though visibly uncertain about the business, Bennett shuffles off to gather up a suit and returns with something in a style akin to Eulalie's own. "I think this oughta fit you well enough, miss." She lays the garments out on the bed. "It's the best I could find."

Exhibiting much less concern for Eulalie's privacy than for Vera Mae's, Bennett stands idly by while Eulalie divests herself of her wet clothes, blissfully unaware that Vera Mae is using the vanity mirror to have a furtive peep. And Vera Mae sees *everything*.

Her breath trapped in her lungs, she stares open-mouthed as Eulalie takes off her camisole, freeing her pert attractions. She has no need of a corset, but she's by no means chicken-breasted. Each perfect handful juts out proudly from her chest, ornamented with small ruby tips.

Her trousers come off next. She tears them down with her knickers, uncovering a dark shadow of neatly trimmed hair at the apex of her creamy thighs. The sight proves too affecting. Succumbing to diffidence, Vera Mae closes her eyes, not daring to open them again until the rustle of clothing stops, all decency restored.

"Well, that was quite the impromptu adventure." She admires Eulalie in the old suit, pleased with how well it fits, even though the loose waistcoat obscures her feminine assets. "It'll take a short while for your clothes to be dried, so will you stay and have some tea with me?"

"I would like that very much." Eulalie opens the door for her. "Lead the way."

Five minutes later, they're seated in the drawing room with a pot of hot tea and a tray of biscuits and cakes. Temporarily uncorseted, Vera Mae makes the most of being able to sit however she pleases and tucks her feet up on the sofa, heels to bum.

"I like you this way." Eulalie approves of the change in her demeanor. "Relaxed and smiling." She tucks a fallen lock of damp hair behind Vera Mae's ear, admiring her features. "You're such a beautiful woman."

"I suppose you see many in your line of work."

"Indeed, but none so beautiful as you." Eulalie caresses her cheek. "Is it terribly improper for me to say so?"

Vera Mae giggles. "I think we've already ventured a little beyond the realms of appropriate behavior with one another, haven't we?" She nuzzles the palm of Eulalie's hand. "What is it that you like about me? Do tell."

Eulalie inches closer. "Absolutely everything." She tiptoes her fingertips over the landmarks of Vera Mae's face. "Your eyes, your nose, your mouth." She brushes her thumb along Vera Mae's soft, full lips, coaxing them to part. "Such delicious lips." She fixes her eyes there and tilts her head, moving in for a kiss ...

"Vera, where are you?" Reginald's booming voice announces his presence seconds before he enters the drawing room.

Recoiling from Eulalie in a panicked flash, Vera Mae swings her legs off the sofa and sits up straight, her foot knocking against the coffee table and sending the multi-tiered cake tray toppling over, biscuits and cakes scattering like bomb debris all over the rug.

"Clumsy fool." Reginald scowls at the mess. "Whatever did you do that for?" He spots Eulalie and the scowl sets in deeper. "Who the devil are you?" He takes in her appearance. "*What* the devil are you?"

"Don't be an arse." Vera Mae rises, smoothing the creases out of her dress. "This is Miss Sauvage, the artist who's painting me. She is my guest, and you will treat her with respect."

At the uncharacteristic use of coarse language, Reginald turns his disapproval upon Vera Mae instead, but she offers no apology.

"It's a pleasure to meet you, milord." Eulalie attempts to placate him by extending her hand, but he doesn't accept it.

"What in God's name are you wearing, woman?"

"We got caught in the rain earlier." Vera Mae comes to Eulalie's defense. "Her clothes were wet, so I had Bennett dig out one of your cousin's old suits." She lays a hand on Eulalie's shoulder, giving her a reassuring squeeze. "This is her preferred style of dress."

"It is *not* a dress, which is exactly my point." Reginald seethes at the casual closeness between them. "Remove your hand from her at once."

"Why?" Vera Mae challenges him. "Is she contagious? You're being ridiculous." She stays put, turning her attention to Eulalie. "Would you like to join us for dinner? You'd be most welcome."

"It's very kind of you to offer, milady, but I really ought to be going."

"Then I shall walk you out." Vera Mae shows her to the front door, stepping onto the porch with her for a few stolen moments of privacy before parting. "Please excuse His Lordship's manner. He is not a tolerant man."

"Him and many others." Eulalie shrugs it off. "I shall return the clothes by first post."

"Don't. Keep them." Vera Mae straightens Eulalie's collar and necktie. "I have no need of them, and they look lovely on you. You're very dashing." She tinkers with Eulalie's lapels purely to prolong their contact. "There's something missing, though."

An idea striking her, she plucks a single violet—a symbol of sapphic love—from a large planter of colorful blooms beside the door and tucks the stem through the buttonhole of Eulalie's new jacket, fixing it in place with a pearl-tipped hairpin teased from her up-do.

"There." She admires her handiwork. "All better."

Forgetting for a moment that a woman's form lurks behind the slightly baggy waistcoat, she lays her hands flat on Eulalie's chest, only realizing her mistake when her palms are cupped around a pair of very womanly breasts.

"Forgive me." She withdraws. "I do believe I've quite forgotten how to be proper." A slight flush pinkens her cheeks. "You appear to have an exceptionally disarming effect upon me."

Eulalie snatches up her retreating hands and kisses her manicured fingers. "I hope that's not a complaint."

"Not a bit of one." Vera Mae relishes every second of skin-to-skin touch. "When will I see you again?" Hearing a noise on the other side of the door and fearing an eavesdropper, she hastily rewords the question. "I mean, when will you return to complete the portrait?"

"Perhaps you might pay me a visit at my studio for the next session?" Eulalie suggests. "The lighting is preferable, and there will be no unwanted interruptions."

Vera Mae agrees readily to that, promises to have her art supplies—along with her dried clothes—sent to her immediately, and they part with a restrained kiss on the cheek. When she steps back inside, she's not terribly surprised to see Reginald loitering in the hall.

"Why are you lurking?"

"I don't care for that woman," he grumbles. "She's irregular."

"Did I invite your opinion?" Vera Mae hasn't the energy to argue with him. "I'm exhausted. Send Bennett up to me when it's time for dinner. I'm going to lie down and read."

She helps herself to a book in from the library—*The Complete Works of Edgar Allan Poe*—and retreats to her bedroom for privacy. After getting herself settled on the bed, she scans the contents for a poem of a particular name: Eulalie.

"Aha!" She finds it, flips to the page, and reads softly to herself. "I dwelt alone in a world of moan, and my soul was a stagnant tide till the fair and gentle Eulalie became my blushing bride ... till the yellow-haired young Eulalie became my smiling bride."

Sighing with longing, she lays the book down. The sacred place between her thighs—a place she's never touched—feels unusually hot and moist, and it's been in that state since she sat down in the drawing room with Eulalie.

Could it be that time of the month already? She counts the days in her head. It doesn't add up. Confused, she navigates a hand inside her knickers and swipes the tip of her index finger along her drenched slit. She expects to pull back her hand and find her digit smeared with crimson, but instead ... nothing. Her fingertip is coated in a mysterious translucent fluid. Arousal? She sucks it onto her tongue, tasting the sweet tang of her sex.

"Oh, God help me." She pushes the book aside and groans into her pillow. "I need her."

CHAPTER

Wednesday June 11, 1913

ON THE MORNING OF THE NEXT SITTING, VERA MAE surprises Bennett by rising early of her own accord and dressing herself, opting for a gauzy pink blouse and matching skirt, her favorite underwear and finest stockings concealed beneath. She adds a little tinted paste to her lips, giving them a glossy sheen, but there's no need for any rouge; excitement alone is responsible for the rosy blush coloring her cheeks.

After hurrying through breakfast, she engages the chauffeur to deliver her to the address on Eulalie's trade card: a modest rented studio nestled on the boundaries of Soho and Mayfair, in the vicinity of Regent Street. It's an area populated by artists of all creative persuasions, including stage performers, painters, writers, and musicians, and has become something of a safe haven for those interested in pursuing a more unconventional way of life. In other words, homosexuals are welcomed without prejudice.

Just a stone's throw from all manner of excitements in Piccadilly Circus, this thriving bohemian community has come a long way from the iniquitous quarter it was known for being in the last century, populated then by rather more unwholesome characters, a vast number of whom were cheap prostitutes. Still, for all its improvements, it's not a place for the aristocracy.

Vera Mae feels the eyes of inquisitive passersby judging her as she steps out of her motorcar in front of Eulalie's building. The enormous property—no doubt once a single private home—is now divided up into various different rental spaces. The brass plates beside the main entrance list no less than three artists, a photographer, a dance instructor, a talent agent, and an animal trainer.

The street door is always open, so Vera Mae wanders in and makes her way through the wide open lobby and up the winding staircase to the second floor. There, she finds Eulalie's name on another brass plate beside studio number nine, and knocks.

She's a bundle of nervous energy but hides it well, even when Eulalie answers wearing only a paint-splattered shirt from the waist up, her unrestrained breasts clearly visible behind the pale cotton, the top buttons undone, baring her neck and a glimpse of her upper chest.

"Come in." Eulalie beckons her inside. "I was just getting everything set up. May I take your jacket?"

Vera Mae takes off her gloves first, tucks them in her pockets, then removes her red, fur-trimmed jacket, revealing the form-fitting pink blouse she selected especially for this moment, hoping Eulalie might approve of the way it clings to her body. And she does.

"You look incredible, milady. As always."

Vera Mae cringes. "Please, enough of the formality between us. Will you call me Vera?"

"If you'll call me Lollie."

"It's settled, then." Vera Mae smiles, drops a kiss on her cheek to seal the deal, then takes a moment to explore the studio.

The large windows are all open, net curtains billowing in the breeze, a constant airflow preventing the stench of paint from overwhelming the senses. Paintings are hung everywhere, and the white walls are lined with canvases in varying degrees of completion, several draped with old sheets.

"Why are some covered?" Vera Mae wonders.

"They are a little risqué." Eulalie chuckles. "I didn't want to offend you."

Intrigued, Vera Mae tugs a sheet off one at random, unveiling a portrait of a nude woman. Painted in the style of the Rokeby Venus by Diego Velázquez, now hanging in the National Gallery, the woman's bare back and buttocks are directly exposed to the onlooker while her face, breasts, and everything below are exposed in the reflection of a mirror.

"Oh, my goodness gracious." Vera Mae raises an eyebrow, her eyes pinned to the dark mound of untamed curls between the woman's slightly parted thighs. "You have certainly captured every detail of her."

"I have a great appreciation for the female form." Eulalie comes to her side. "You could say that it's a passion of mine."

"Who are your subjects?" Vera Mae uncovers another nude.

"Some are private commissions. It's becoming quite the usual thing for women of your class to request a private portrait to hang in their boudoir. But others ..." Eulalie whisks a sheet away from a large canvas at the far end of the room, this one depicting three naked women pleasuring one another on a large bed. "Others, I paint for my own personal enjoyment and later sell them. These women are ... not women of your caliber, shall we say."

Vera Mae knows what that means. "They're whores."

"Some make a very fine living as artists' models."

"I don't doubt it." Vera Mae turns her attention to a second room divided from the studio by a heavy curtain. In it, there's a double bed. The linens are crumpled and displaced, as if recently used. "You sleep here?"

57

"It's convenient." Eulalie tosses the discarded sheets into a corner, covering a curious phallic object attached to leather straps. "I work late, often keeping odd hours. In any case, what more does a person need? A place to sit"—she indicates a large sofa in the middle of the studio—"a place to eat"—she motions to a cluttered table by one of the windows—"a place to sleep, and if you're lucky, someone to sleep with."

Vera Mae gazes wistfully at the bed. "I've always slept alone. My late husband believed that a woman had but one purpose in the bedroom, and once that duty was tended to, he saw no reason to linger." Disinclined to dwell on that topic, she turns away from the bedroom area, her eyes landing upon a disorganized heap of women's suffrage pamphlets on the table.

Amongst the spread is a copy of Monday morning's *Times* newspaper open to a page announcing the sad death of suffragette Emily Wilding Davison on the afternoon of June 8.

"There's been a lot going on these last few days." Eulalie follows her eyeline. "I'm sorry I wasn't able to make this appointment with you sooner."

"I understand." Vera Mae skims the article, learning that Emily died peacefully, having never regained consciousness. "She was there that day at the suffragette fair, wasn't she? I saw her saluting Joan of Arc." She flips the newspaper over, not wanting to read any more of the dismal details. "What was she attempting to do at the Derby? The papers are all painting her as a mad woman, saying it serves her damn well right. I don't believe a word of it."

"She was trying to affix a 'Votes for Women' scarf to the horse's bridle." Eulalie sighs, shaking her head. "I warned her against it, but she wanted the King's horse to cross the finishing line wearing suffragette colors."

Vera Mae hears disapproval in her tone. "You don't approve of such reckless tactics?"

"Not often." Eulalie overturns another newspaper reporting the destruction of Hurst Park Racecourse stand in an arson attack committed by two suffragettes on the evening of Emily's death. "I attend all WSPU demonstrations and rallies, and have many friends who remain fiercely loyal to the Pankhursts, but I am not such an active participant in the campaign of militancy as I once was."

"Ah, so you are not a suffragette, but a suffragist." Vera Mae pinpoints the subtle difference. "You are a pacifist."

"Most days." Eulalie shrugs. "Certainly I've come to align myself more with the Women's Freedom League." She hands Vera Mae a copy of *The Vote*, a suffrage newspaper published by the League. "We oppose violence. We'd rather organize peaceful protests and chain ourselves to furniture in the Houses of Parliament than go about smashing windows and setting fire to pillar boxes. Sadly, it seems the only language men recognize is the language of war, so perhaps Emmeline Pankhurst has been right all along: No measure worth having has been won in any other way."

Vera Mae flicks through the magazine. "You know, I was once caught in the crossfire of a WSPU protest. A few termagants wearing suffragette sashes barged their way into a party I was attending with Reginald and set about hurling various fruit projectiles at any political men they could find. I happened to be standing a shade too close to someone bearing the Asquith name and my lovely new dress got splattered by an errant tomato." She brings a hand to her breast. "Right in the bosom."

Unable to stifle it, Eulalie guffaws. "I'm sorry, but I suppose that's the risk you take these days when keeping company with people who oppose women's rights."

"In my circles, it's rather difficult to avoid such people," Vera Mae laments. "Most members of the aristocracy abhor the very notion of modernization. Especially those who hover somewhat uneasily on the less comfortable edge of the class. It terrifies them. They live in perpetual fear of it."

"And you?"

"I know the world is changing, and I won't stand in its way. I am of a dying breed. I shan't glue myself obstinately to the past. Better to embrace things as they come."

"Says the woman still lacing herself into a corset every morning." Eulalie roves her eyes over Vera Mae's perfect body. "You know there is a new fangled thing called a brassiere. It's much more liberating."

"Perhaps I'm old-fashioned, but I like the way a corset makes me feel." Vera Mae runs a hand down her armored ribcage. "Do you not like the way it makes me look? I heard no objection from you when you were ogling me in my bedroom." She faces Eulalie head on. "Feel the form of it beneath my clothes."

At invitation, Eulalie lays her hands on Vera Mae's hips, at the lowest point of the corset, and glides them upwards, following the dip into her narrowed waist then over her ribs, coming to a stop beneath her breasts.

"You have the most exquisite form." Eulalie settles her hands back on Vera Mae's hips. "But I'm quite sure that has very little to do with the corset. It's all you." She ventures over Vera Mae's rump and gives her buttocks a firm squeeze, eliciting a delighted squeak.

"Your portrait is nearly finished, by the way." She returns both wandering paws to Vera Mae's waist. "Would you like to see it?"

"You've completed it from memory?" Vera Mae claps her hands together. "How frightfully clever."

Eulalie guides her to the wet canvas on an easel by the window, positioned to steal the best daylight. "What do you think?"

Vera Mae gasps. Gone is the demure woman with an air of melancholia about her. In her place is an amorous woman wearing a red silk gown, sprawled barefoot on a chaise surrounded by roses. A woman with ample cleavage, her dress eased suggestively off one shoulder, her flirtatious eyes looking straight out of the painting—straight at the artist.

"If it's too indecent, I shall paint another," Eulalie offers.

"No." Vera Mae shakes her head vehemently. "I like it. I like the way you see me." She pinches her lower lip between her teeth, comparing the figure of her painted self with her reflection in a nearby cheval mirror. "Am I really so ... sensual?"

Eulalie swoops in behind her, joining in the scrutiny of her body. "Absolutely." She drops a featherlight kiss on Vera Mae's neck. "Every inch of you."

Vera Mae mewls, goose bumps pricking her skin. "I've never known a woman like you."

"Like me in what way?" Another kiss.

"You know very well what way." Vera Mae tilts her head, presenting more of her neck for Eulalie's lips. "And you should know that I'm a ... a novice." She feels silly saying it. "You're stirring things in me, Lollie. Things I haven't felt in a long time. Things I thought were dormant in me."

Eulalie halts her kisses. "Does it frighten you?"

"A little," Vera Mae confesses. "You must understand, I've never had true intimacy."

"But your husband ..."

Vera Mae grimaces. "My husband invited himself into my bed only when he felt inspired to exercise his marital rights, which thankfully wasn't all that often. And the best way I can describe that pitiful business is to say that he rutted on me like a wild dog until reaching the inevitable crisis of his pleasure, at which point his language would become quite foul. When he was done, he'd thank me and return to his own room. Is that intimacy? I think not."

"I'm sorry." Eulalie rubs the tension out of her shoulders. "Your needs have never been tended?"

"Not once." Vera Mae relaxes under Eulalie's tender ministrations. "Not even by my own hand." Ashamed of her inexperience, she breaks her eyes away from Eulalie's in the mirror, unable to maintain eye contact. "You must think me so frigid."

"Not frigid. Neglected." Eulalie spins her around and pulls her into an embrace. "It's a travesty that you've had to suffer such loneliness, and I vow to you now that if you see fit to trust me with your love, I will do everything in my power to make you the happiest woman who's ever walked the Earth." She lowers her voice to a whisper. "In and out of bed."

Vera Mae groans. Beneath her many layers of clothing, the core of her body pulses with lust, her knickers dampen, and she quivers.

"Your words are having such a devastating effect upon me." She sinks into Eulalie's arms. "But let's not rush." She tries to ignore the rhythmic throbbing between her thighs. "Make love to me. Court me. Woo me. And take me out to tea."

"Tea?" Eulalie queries. "Right now?"

Vera Mae nods. "This very minute. I am parched."

CHAPTER

IT'S ONLY A TEN MINUTE ARM-IN-ARM WALK FROM EULALIE'S studio to Selfridges department store on Oxford Street—an establishment of Vera Mae's choosing. She's been to the store's fashionable Palm Court Restaurant countless times. It's known to be frequented by the wealthy and famous, and isn't exactly a place where one can easily remain inconspicuous.

Mere yards away from the main entrance, Eulalie brings her to a halt. "Are you sure you wouldn't rather take tea with me at the Criterion Restaurant?" She names a place in Piccadilly Circus that's a regular spot for members of the WSPU to conduct their afternoon meetings. "I know what a great risk it is for you to be seen with someone like me, and I fear that if we enter Selfridges together, we will surely be noticed by someone of influence."

"Then let them see." Vera Mae hugs her arm tighter. "I do not fear the wagging tongues and disapproving glares of my peers. Why ought I be ashamed?" She steps in front of Eulalie, fussing with the newly tailored outfit donated from her late husband's wardrobe. "You do look ever so handsome in this suit. Much more so than the man who formerly occupied it, God rest his soul." She runs her hands down Eulalie's chest, the waistcoat now fitted to her form. "Your tailor's done a very good job."

She pokes her finger through the empty buttonhole where her flower once was, nothing left of that day but the pearl-tipped hairpin. Seeking to remedy that, she hails a passing flower girl, buys a single red rose from her basket of flowers, and fixes it in place. As she's doing so, a couple of middle-aged women walk by muttering derogatory comments about Eulalie. One calls her an invert, the other condemns her as disgusting.

Vera Mae opens her mouth to give them a sharp education in proper British manners, but Eulalie puts a finger to her lips and stops her.

"Don't." She squeezes Vera Mae's hand. "I appreciate the place in your heart that reaction comes from, but they aren't worth a fight."

"How can you abide such rudeness?" Vera Mae huffs.

"It's something you learn to ignore." Eulalie calms her. "My unconventional appearance doesn't always make for a good first impression. Especially among people of your quality." She spins the topic in a more positive direction. "What did you think when you first saw me? Be honest."

Vera Mae smiles, all tension erased. "You bewitched me. I thought you were bold, beautiful, and so very beguiling. Of course then I was immediately jealous because you had your arm around another woman." The smile turns into a theatrical pout. "I'm surprised you noticed me at all."

"You caught my eye the moment you walked in," Eulalie assures her. "You were the most gorgeous woman in the room."

"I'm glad you pursued me." Vera Mae starts walking toward Selfridges. "Now, if you want me, you must pursue me again. Straight into the Palm Court."

Eulalie does as she's told, and they soon become the center of attention in the terrace restaurant. People gawp, people smirk, and Vera Mae ignores them all. They order a pot of tea and some sandwiches, and soon the rest of the world fades away. Until Harry Selfridge walks in.

"Oh, look, there he is." Vera Mae points out the mustached owner of Selfridges to Eulalie. "Mr. Selfridge himself."

Eulalie turns to look, catches his eye, and waves.

"Miss Sauvage!" He recognizes her at once, whisks off his top hat, tucks his ornamental walking stick under his arm, and strides over to greet her. "What a great pleasure it is to see you here." His soft American accent contrasts sharply with those around him. "And in such dazzling company." He turns his winning smile on Vera Mae.

"May I present my good friend Lady Vera Mae Darlington." Eulalie facilitates the introduction. "She's a big fan of your store."

"I'm glad to hear it." He bends to kiss Vera Mae's hand. "I hope Miss Sauvage is treating you well? Whatever you want is on the house today. Do enjoy yourselves, ladies."

He excuses himself to other business and as soon as he's gone, Vera Mae balls up her napkin and throws it at Eulalie in mock outrage.

"How do you know Mr. Selfridge? And why did you not tell me?"

"I painted his wife's portrait." Eulalie laughs. "I didn't know it was relevant."

"Well, here I thought I was bringing you somewhere to impress you, yet it is you who's ended up impressing me. Well played, Miss Sauvage." Vera Mae takes back her napkin. "Where did you learn to paint anyway? You really are very good."

"I spent a few years in Paris."

"Is that where you acquired the name Sauvage?"

"It is." Eulalie volunteers nothing.

"And before that?" Vera Mae tries to tease more information out of her, but she remains deliberately and infuriatingly vague.

"A different name, a different life." Eulalie brushes it off as nothing of importance. "May I ask you about the man you live with? Who is he?"

"He is my late husband's cousin."

"And what is his place?"

Vera Mae nurses her teacup, pondering the meaning of the question. "With me? Or with the barony and the estate? Not that they're entirely separate, I suppose." She sets her teacup down. "Since my husband died without a male heir, the estate passed to Reginald along with the title. If I do not marry him, I will cease to belong." She stares into the bottom of her cup. "To tell you the truth, I already feel as though I am a tenant in my own home, and my lease is fast expiring."

"Nothing of it is yours?"

"Sadly not." Vera Mae sighs. "All I ever had became the property of my husband upon our marriage. You know how these things work. Every penny of mine was put into the estate. That was the purpose of his marrying me after all."

"What was your purpose in marrying him?" Eulalie pries deeper.

"Obligation." Vera Mae knows how pathetic that sounds. "I am the youngest daughter of an earl. My family only ever had one expectation of me: to marry, so that the burden of supporting my existence in this mortal sphere could be passed off on someone else. When I reached the grand old age of twenty-six and had not yet wedded, it became a matter of some desperation. So I did as they wished and married a baron."

"At the expense of your happiness?"

"That's how I was raised." Vera Mae imparts the cold truth of it. "And one does eventually grow accustomed to the inherent discontent that comes from living a life such as mine. Resistance is futile. Apathy is inevitable."

As Eulalie reaches for her hand across the table, offering solace, a woman approaches their quiet corner of the Palm Court and greets Vera Mae with a forced smile, her interruption promptly curtailing all flirtations.

She appears friendly enough on the surface but proceeds to throw disdainful looks Eulalie's way at every opportunity, soon making it glaringly apparent that she only brought herself over for the purpose of gathering gossip. To that end, Vera Mae gives her precisely what she wants and steers the conversation straight into salacious territory.

"This is Miss Eulalie Sauvage. She's a very accomplished artist."

"Really?" The woman, who refuses to acknowledge Eulalie directly, sounds doubtful. "What sort of thing does she paint?"

"Nudes." Vera Mae pauses to let that sink in, then goes on to ensure the woman's swift departure. "I'm posing for Miss Sauvage this afternoon as a matter of fact. Would you like to join us? There's always room for one more."

Predictably shocked and horrified by that outlandish proposition, the woman concocts an excuse to cut the conversation short and makes a hasty escape, leaving Vera Mae with a smug smile on her face and Eulalie in a state of dazed, awestruck astonishment.

"You are one sassy baroness today." Eulalie marvels at her. "You quite surprise me."

"I hope that's not a complaint." Vera Mae winks, rubbing her ankle against Eulalie's leg beneath the table. "Shall we order some cake?"

That's rhetorical. She sees to it that a selection of miniature cakes is brought to their table along with a fresh pot of tea, and they take their time in the Palm Court. In no hurry to depart from one another, they continue their date with an arm-in-arm stroll through Soho, perusing the various shops and entertainments until eventually ambling back to Eulalie's studio.

"Will you come inside?" Eulalie asks as they arrive at the street door.

"I have to go." Vera Mae holds back.

"You *have* to?"

"On this occasion, yes." Vera Mae lays her hands on Eulalie's chest again, this time without embarrassment. "I mustn't be late for dinner. My absence would cause trouble, and I'm not yet ready for trouble."

"I will let you go if I must." Eulalie steps closer, pressing Vera Mae's hands more firmly over her breasts. "But I hope you'll visit me again soon."

"I couldn't keep away if I tried." Vera Mae massages her over the waistcoat. "I like the way you make me feel, Lollie. It terrifies me, but I promise you I will not shy from it. I have shied from things my whole life and will do so no longer."

In parting, Eulalie drops a tender kiss on her lips. Just a peck, nothing more. Their lips meet for the briefest of moments before Eulalie hails a passing hackney carriage to take her back to the Regent's Park house—a journey which Vera Mae spends in a state of delirium.

Her lips tingle with the memory of Eulalie's kiss, chaste though it was, and she's in high spirits when she strides into the library in search of money to pay the carriage fare.

"Do you have any coins?" she asks of Reginald, finding him sipping a glass of whiskey by the fireplace.

He grunts something incoherent. "What for?"

"I have to pay the cab man." She roots through a drawer in the bureau, discovering it to be a dumping ground for coins of all denominations.

"You've been spending time with that confounded artist." Reginald manages to make that statement sound an awful lot like an accusation.

"Yes. Why?" Vera Mae faces him defiantly, primed for a quarrel. "Who told you?"

"You were seen at Selfridges." He expects her to be apologetic.

"Is that a crime?" She sends the butler away with enough money to pay the carriage.

"It ought to be. That Sauvage woman is one of those wretched ... inverts." Reginald snarls out the word. "Even worse, she's a damn suffragette."

"Suffragist," Vera Mae corrects him.

68

"Don't be pedantic," he snaps at her. "I don't want you mixed in with that kind of woman. I forbid you to see her again."

"You *forbid* me?!" Vera Mae abandons her docility. "How dare you!" Lacking a better weapon, she hurls her gloves in his direction, missing him by a wide margin. "May I remind you that you are *not* my husband."

He says more, but she doesn't hear it. She storms from the library and shuts herself in her room, refusing to go down for dinner, her good mood crushed.

CHAPTER

Saturday June 14, 1913

BREAKFAST WITH REGINALD IS BECOMING INCREASINGLY insufferable. If he's not making unfavorable comments about the women's suffrage movement, he's making them about Eulalie.

"How much longer before this silly little portrait of yours is finished?" he asks between mouthfuls of scrambled eggs, his fork in one hand, this morning's newspaper in the other.

"Soon." Vera Mae picks at her food. "A few more sessions. It's almost done."

"Good." Reginald sets down the newspaper in favor of the latest issue of *The Anti Suffrage Review*. "You're spending far too much time with that invert."

Vera Mae slams down her cutlery. "Will you please stop calling her that?"

"Don't tell me you have a sympathy for the sort?" Reginald snorts.

"Perhaps I do." Vera Mae reaches across the table and helps herself to his discarded newspaper. "Are you done with this?"

Taken aback by her audacity, Reginald gawks at her. "Whatever's gotten into you?"

"Nothing." Vera Mae conceals a wicked smile behind the newspaper. "The coconut's not yet been breached."

"I beg your pardon?" Reginald frowns so deeply his eyebrows meet in the middle of his forehead. "You're talking utter nonsense, woman. What's wrong with you?"

"I'm perfectly well, thank you." Vera Mae keeps reading. "Never been better."

"I'd query that." Reginald's frown sticks. "Are your female troubles on again? Or has that bloody invert been rubbing off on you?"

Vera Mae titters. She tries to bite it back, but it escapes. "Rubbing off on me ... honestly, Reginald, you're being ever so vulgar."

"For goodness sake, Vera." Reginald throws his magazine down, exasperated. "What in God's name is going on? Have you been drinking?"

"Oh, forget it." Vera Mae abandons the newspaper. "I've had enough of this." She tosses her napkin on the table and gets up. "I'm going for a walk."

She leaves him perplexed and departs from the Regent's Park house without further word, heading straight for Eulalie's studio. Along the way, she loses count of the number of women she sees proudly displaying their suffragette colors, many wearing purple or green skirts coupled with white muslin blouses. They're traveling in throngs, filling the streets and pavements, some carrying placards.

Deeds, not words!

Justice for women!

One carries a large black flag painted with the words 'Liberty or death!'.

Is there a protest? A rally? Vera Mae has no idea. She weaves her way through them, refusing to be waylaid, and arrives at the studio just as Eulalie is leaving with two other women.

Both women are dressed in white, their outfits adorned with WSPU sashes and hats, and they see her ascending the staircase before Eulalie does.

"Ay up, who's this proper swank piece of skirt?" One eyes her from the landing.

Eulalie, herself adorned with the red, white, and green colors of the National Union of Women's Suffrage Societies, turns to look. "Vera! I didn't get a message that you were coming."

"I didn't telephone." Vera Mae hesitates at the top of the stairs. "It was silly of me. I'm sorry to have called upon you unannounced." She turns to leave.

"No, no, no." Eulalie catches her arm and holds her back. "Don't go. It's Emily's funeral today, and we're just on our way to pay our respects. Come with us."

Vera Mae shakes her head. "No, I ..."

"Come with us," Eulalie insists. "Please."

"I don't want to intrude."

"It's no intrusion." Eulalie squeezes her gloved hand. "I want you with me." For added reassurance, she backs Vera Mae against the wall and plants a tender kiss on her lips—right in front of their suffragette audience.

"Oooh!" The taller of the goggling pair coos. "Aintcha gonna introduce us to your new honey, Lollie?" She plants her hands on her hips, affronted.

"Looks like our Lollie's acquired some expensive taste," the shorter suffragette chimes in. "Worst luck for you." She snickers at her tall comrade's expense.

"Ignore them." Eulalie apologizes to Vera Mae on behalf of her friends. "They lack manners." She points at the tall one. "That's Kitty." And the short one. "That's Connie." She keeps Vera Mae held against the wall and lowers her voice. "How would you like to be introduced?"

"I'm Vera," Vera Mae introduces herself. "It's a very great pleasure to meet you both."

"Well, ain't you all refined and formal like." Kitty scrutinizes her expensive clothing. "I reckon I smell the pungent aroma of the aristocracy on you, my love. Am I right?"

Vera Mae hangs her head, unable to deny it.

"Too prim and proper for your own good, you lot are." Kitty shoves past them and heads down the staircase. "Not to my taste, and that's a fact."

Connie scurries after her. "Pay no notice," she whispers to Vera Mae on the way. "Kitty's a jealous one, that's all."

"Jealous?" Vera Mae feels a prick of that herself and draws Eulalie closer. "Have you bedded her?"

"The dalliance has passed."

"She wishes it had not."

"But it has nonetheless." Eulalie takes Vera Mae by the chin, tilts her head up, and kisses her again, this time keeping their lips pinched together for several seconds. "I'm glad you're here."

The short walk to Bloomsbury, where the funeral procession organized by the NUWSS is scheduled to pass, is peppered with talk of Emily Wilding Davison's ultimate sacrifice for the cause and the high price of liberty. While Kitty strides on ahead in a sulk, Connie recounts that Emily always believed some desperate protest—one great tragedy—might well be a catalyst for reform, bringing women one step closer to equal rights and spelling the end of the harsh imprisonments so many suffragettes are subjected to. She thought the crusade needed a martyr, and she became one.

"The glorious and inscrutable spirit of liberty has but one further penalty within its power: the surrender of life itself." Connie recites from a passage Emily wrote in a suffrage publication last year. "To lay down life for friends—that is glorious, selfless, inspiring! And she will not shrink from this nirvana. She will be faithful to the last."

With a sniffle, Connie pulls a hanky from her pocket and blows her nose. "I visited her in the hospital. She had such horrid letters of hate sent to her as she lay there dying. You wouldn't believe some of the things. One said: Miss Davison, I am glad to hear you are in hospital. I hope you suffer torture until you die. I consider you are a person unworthy of existence in this world, and should like the opportunity of starving and beating you to a pulp." She shakes her head in despair. "People's so dreadful, ain't they?"

The closer they get to Bloomsbury, the more densely packed the streets become. People are pooling in from all directions, swarming together. Tens of thousands of people—men, women, and children—are clamoring for a glimpse of the procession, many wearing the colors of the various suffrage unions to which they belong. It's a turbulent sea of bobbing hats.

One woman, dressed as Joan of Arc, stands on a chair and preaches Emmeline Pankhurst's most recent exaltation: "Be militant each in your own way. Those of you who can break windows, break them. Those of you who can further attack the sacred idol of property, do so. Carry on the holy war for the emancipation of our sex!"

On the periphery of the rapidly swelling masses, Vera Mae's anxiety erupts. People are cramming together like sardines, jostling for position, shoulders bumping, bodies grinding, pressing, and shoving. The biggest and the strongest barge through. Suffragettes carrying placards demand their place up front.

The noise is tremendous. Individual sounds become indistinguishable in the cacophony of crying babies, incessant chatter, and chanting suffragettes. Vera Mae struggles to breathe. The ground feels uneven beneath her feet, as if she's standing on the deck of a listing ship, and she stumbles, grabbing onto Eulalie for support.

"I can't, I can't, I can't ..." She pulls back toward the fringes of the mob.

"Yes, you can." Eulalie draws her into an embrace. "Close your eyes." She holds Vera Mae to her chest. "Breathe slow. I've got you in my arms."

Vera Mae presses herself to Eulalie, feeling the steady, rhythmic beating of her heart. "Don't let me go."

"I won't." Eulalie rubs her back. "I won't ever let you go, I promise. I shall be right here with you. Nothing will hurt you." She waits until Vera Mae's breathing normalizes, then coaxes her to take a few steps. "I'll protect you."

Vera Mae clutches Eulalie's arm so hard her nails dig into flesh, and they move deeper into the throngs. While Kitty and Connie push their way to the very front of the masses, Eulalie finds a vantage point atop the steps of a goods warehouse set back from the street, where fewer people are congregated.

"How's this?" She stands behind Vera Mae, shielding her from anyone who might accidentally knock into her. "Do you feel all right?" She wraps both arms around Vera Mae's middle, holding her securely, enveloping her in warmth. "Do you feel safe?"

Vera Mae is surprised to say that she does. Her erratic breathing is under control, her heart doesn't feel as though it's about to rupture, and Eulalie is being the perfect gentleman. By the time the procession snakes by, her nerves are completely in check. Not gone, but manageable.

Though the atmosphere is one of sorrow, there's a prevailing sense of unity. Thousands of suffragettes follow the coffin and many more are leading the way. All are wearing white dresses and hats, sashes in suffrage colors, and black armbands of mourning, many of them wielding decorated wreaths and banners.

She hath done what she could.

Give me liberty, or give me death!

Fight on, and God will give the victory.

The coffin itself is on a low bier pulled by four black horses. It's covered with a purple, silver-edged silk pall topped with three laurel wreaths and a poignant inscription reading: She died for women.

"Was it worth it?" Vera Mae wonders as the somber procession passes by. "Such an extreme act of defiance."

"We will never come to rest. Not until women are equal to men in all regards." Eulalie keeps her eyes on the coffin till it disappears out of sight, moving on toward Euston Station. "Millicent Fawcett, president of the NUWSS, says our movement is like a glacier: slow moving but unstoppable."

When all's said and done, Kitty and Connie flock together with a group of their WSPU comrades and head to the Criterion Restaurant to celebrate Emily's life, but Eulalie declines the invite, waits for the throngs to disperse, and walks Vera Mae back to her studio. Inside, the sofa has been pushed to the edge of the room, the center of the floor spread with soft furnishings, creating a padded bed of cushions, throw pillows, and blankets. It looks like a scene from a brothel.

"What went on here?" Vera Mae finds a series of pornographic photographs on the table, each one depicting the same two nude women sprawled on the heap, positioned in a creative array of erotic poses. "Is this work or play?"

Chuckling, Eulalie strips off her jacket, waistcoat, and tie, and flops onto the pile. "Private collectors pay handsomely for bespoke pornography. It is rather good fun—I shan't lie about that—but I do it all for work, I promise." She invites Vera Mae to join her. "You've nothing to worry about. You're the only woman I want."

Vera Mae lowers herself onto the cushions, envious of how easily Eulalie can move without the restriction of a corset. "Once I get down, I may never get back up."

She settles into Eulalie's waiting arms, tucks herself against Eulalie's body, and soon welcomes a kiss. But this kiss is different. All chaste tenderness is gone, and Vera Mae feels Eulalie's tongue entreating for entry into her mouth. On the next assault, their tongues meet, caressing briefly before retreating. And again. Again. Again ...

Breaking for air, Vera Mae rolls onto her back and whimpers at the ceiling. "I never knew a kiss could be so lewd." She catches her breath and snuggles back into Eulalie's arms. "Wherever did you learn such a wicked thing?"

"That's how they do it in France."

Vera Mae giggles. "Why is everything French always so unspeakably naughty?"

"Because the French know how to enjoy themselves."

Eulalie initiates another round of erotic kisses, and Vera Mae moans into each one, neither one of them paying any attention to the passing of time. When they get hungry, Eulalie sends the landlady's son out to fetch sandwiches and wine. And more wine. Halfway through the second bottle, she brings out her sketchbook and attempts to draw Vera Mae, but her fine motor skills are impaired and Vera Mae is getting bawdy.

Elevated on the booze, she unbuttons her blouse to her bust. "Here, draw me like one of your whores." She peels her blouse and camisole away from her chest, showing a splash of her corset, and reclines on the cushions, adopting a suggestive pose.

Eulalie takes one look at her and tosses the sketchbook over her shoulder. "Forget it. Now I cannot concentrate." With a growl, she dives across the cushions and lowers herself over Vera Mae, dropping kisses on every inch of unclothed skin, paying particular attention to the upper swells of her heaving breasts.

"Do you want more?" She fingers the top clasp of Vera Mae's corset. "Tell me you do."

"You know I do," Vera Mae whispers, a tremor in her voice. "But not tonight." She stays Eulalie's hand, preventing her from undoing the clasp.

Eulalie groans. "Why not? What is it you fear so much that you would deny yourself the pleasure I'm so ready to give you?" She fails to understand and leaps to the worst conclusion. "Is it Reginald? Does he hurt you? If he's ever raised a hand to you, I swear—"

"Hush." Vera Mae silences her. "Stand down, Tigress. It's nothing whatsoever like that." She cups her hands around Eulalie's cheeks. "My fierce, beautiful tigress. Will you be patient? I wish to be courted a little longer, that is all. I want everything to be as perfect as it can possibly be."

Eulalie purrs and nuzzles her palms. "I'm half mad with want of you." She trails the tip of her index finger over Vera Mae's bared bosom. "But I will endeavor to contain myself." She holds Vera Mae's blouse closed, removing temptation from her sight. "For now."

Vera Mae breaks into a smile. "I shan't make you wait long. We're having a small gathering at the house next weekend. Will you come?"

"I will be welcome?"

"You will be my guest—my *honored* guest—and Reginald won't dare cause a fuss in front of his friends."

"You're sure?" Eulalie frets. "And I will not embarrass you? I'm afraid I don't own a dress. I haven't worn one in nearly three years. Not even for special occasions."

"Don't be silly." Vera Mae plants a kiss on her. "I want you just as you are, and I shall be bored to tears if you aren't there."

"All right, I am sufficiently convinced." Eulalie releases her blouse. "Now give me one more peep to tide me over in the meantime." She feasts her eyes. "Maybe just one more kiss ..."

Before they part company, Eulalie gives her a bit more than that. Taking care to do so in a place that won't be seen, even in the most daring evening gown, she bites down on Vera Mae's right breast, scraping her teeth along the delicate virgin flesh, leaving behind a deep purple bruise: a mark of passion.

The mere thought of it—simply knowing that it's there, hiding beneath her clothing—keeps Vera Mae in a heightened state of arousal all the way home. Sadly, her euphoria doesn't last. Reginald obliterates it the moment she walks in.

"That was some walk." He glowers at her. "Where were you?"

"Nowhere that need concern you." She tries to walk past him, but he bars the way.

"If you're up to no good with that—"

"Don't say it." She cuts him off and steps around him, heading for the stairs.

"You'll lose everything," he calls after her. "And you'll no longer be welcome here."

She doesn't even break stride. "Goodnight, Reginald."

CHAPTER

Saturday June 21, 1913

VERA MAE SMILES POLITELY, FEIGNING INTEREST IN THE mundane lives of her guests as they sip pre-dinner drinks in the drawing room. They've been arriving steadily for the last half an hour, but there's only one invitee she has any interest in, and when the butler finally announces Eulalie's arrival, she practically leaps off her chair.

"What is that infernal woman doing here?" Reginald snarls under his breath.

"She is my guest." Vera Mae crosses the library to greet her. "Miss Sauvage, I'm glad you could make it." She presents her gloved hand for shaking.

"My lady." Eulalie kisses the back of her hand, then flips her hand over and kisses her inner wrist.

"Careful," Vera Mae cautions her, standing between her and the rest of the room. "We aren't alone." She leans in close to peck Eulalie's cheek. "More's the pity."

"Miss Sauvage." Reginald startles Vera Mae by sidling up to her, slapping his thick arm around her waist, and making somewhat pleasant conversation.

"How is that ludicrous portrait coming along? It must be such a bore for you. I'm sure Her Ladyship's been frightfully dull company. Not much fun at all."

"On the contrary." Eulalie smirks. "I've been enjoying her company immensely."

Vera Mae flashes Eulalie a coy smile, erasing it from her lips before Reginald catches it. "Why don't you fetch Miss Sauvage a drink?" she suggests, seeking to be rid of him. "I'm sure she'd like one."

"Isn't that what we have footmen for?" He looks around for one.

"Not as many as we used to." Vera Mae sidesteps out of his grasp. "That's the price of modernization, remember?"

Muttering something incoherent, Reginald wanders off in search of someone to do his bidding.

"How can you stand him pawing on you like that?" Eulalie watches him walk away, one of her fists slightly clenched. "As if he has any claim on you."

"Ignore him." Vera Mae slinks up to her and tickles a finger in her palm, coaxing her to relax. "He's showing off. Like a gorilla beating its chest in the jungle."

She wishes she could devote her full attention to Eulalie, but she must play the perfect hostess. From the moment Reginald returns with a drink, there's no opportunity for anything more than a furtive glance or a subtle touch of hands until the dinner gong sounds and they're seated beside one another at the dining room table. Then, between courses, Vera Mae feels Eulalie's hand creep onto her lap, obscured by the tablecloth.

"You're being ever so naughty with me," she whispers.

"No-one can tell." Eulalie squeezes her knee.

"These sorts of people can always tell." Vera Mae tries to behave naturally, though she knows she's blushing furiously. "They have a sixth sense for impropriety. Have even so much as a dirty thought and someone somewhere will surely condemn you for it."

Eulalie withdraws before the desert course.

Shortly after dinner, the women separate from their male counterparts. While the men remain in the dining room, smoking cigars and drinking port, everyone in possession of a uterus retires to the drawing room. And that's when the questions begin.

Freed from the judging eyes of their husbands, Vera Mae's friends want to know all about the curious suffragette artist who dares to wear such odd clothes. They cram onto the sofa with her, fussing around her and pawing on her as if she were an exotic exhibit at the zoo.

"Heavens, give her some air." Vera Mae finds herself relegated to a chair opposite. "You'll suffocate the poor woman."

Her words have no effect. The excited ladies want to know anything and everything.

"How much willful damage have you caused?" one asks in relation to Eulalie's suffragette activities, having absolutely no grasp of the difference between the militant WSPU and other women's suffrage organizations. "Do you keep a tally amongst yourselves? Have you ever been arrested? Do tell us!"

"I'm afraid I only break hearts, not windows, these days." Eulalie answers with a charming smile. "Although, if you'd have asked me not so terribly long ago, the answer would've been quite different."

"How so?" The woman drapes her arm on Eulalie's shoulder, getting much too close for Vera Mae's comfort.

"I used to be a very active member of the WSPU, as was my mother," Eulalie explains. "She'd been involved with the organization since 1906, when the Pankhursts set up their new headquarters here in London, and she brought me into it with her. I was only eighteen then, and proud to call myself a suffragette soldier."

"What changed?" Vera Mae adjusts her pink silk dress, inching it up a little to expose her delicate stockinged ankles, hoping to snare Eulalie's interest. "Why have you drawn away from the WSPU? You've never said."

"As the years went by and the atmosphere within the WSPU became ever more febrile, my mother was arrested several times for committing militant acts." Eulalie's gaze drifts down Vera Mae's body. "She stood strong with her fellow comrades during her imprisonment, went on hunger strike, and was force fed on every occasion. It was barbaric. Twice a day, four wardresses held her down on a chair, put a clamp in her mouth to keep it open, and inserted the feeding tube. If she struggled too much, the tube was put up her nose instead."

"Did she recover?" Vera Mae is the only one to show genuine concern. "I've read of women who've developed many serious health troubles as a result of the hideous treatment they've been subjected to at the hands of the police."

"She battles on, but I'm sorry to say she recently suffered a stroke." Eulalie's gaze drops to the floor. "I believe her heart was weakened by all that she endured."

"Oh, my God ..." Vera Mae rises from her chair, displaces one of the other women, and budges her way onto the sofa. "No wonder you have become a pacifist." She de-gloves herself and takes Eulalie's hand, not caring how the gesture appears to those around them.

"Tell me something, my lady." Eulalie bucks herself up. "Have I any hope of convincing you to attend a peaceful demonstration with me one day? A suffragist pilgrimage began in Land's End two days ago, and is on its way to London as we speak. When it gets here, it'll converge with seventeen other pilgrimages coming from all over England, and there's to be a rally in Hyde Park. You'd be in good company. Lady Constance Lytton is a proud and outspoken supporter of the women's suffrage movement, and she's your people."

"True enough, but I'm afraid Lady Constance is a much braver woman than I." Vera Mae refrains from committing herself to the cause. "You know, my husband once caught me reading one of her women's rights pamphlets and threw the damn thing straight on the fire. He thought it best that I didn't excite myself. He preferred me passive."

"Well, if you'll let me"—Eulalie sandwiches Vera Mae's hands between her own—"I should very much like the opportunity to excite you."

Vera Mae feels a glorious shiver run through her core. "You already do."

She says that without thinking, and their casual flirtation does not escape unnoticed. One woman warns her to be careful while another backs away from the sofa, no doubt able to sense the undercurrent of tension running between them.

"Oh, do calm yourselves." Vera Mae rolls her eyes. "The world shan't come to an end on the heels of a little coquetry between two women. Are you really all such prudes?"

Silence.

"I suppose you are, then." She sighs and gets up, unconcerned. "Come with me, Miss Sauvage." She holds her hand out to Eulalie. "I shall take you on a tour of the house, since these ladies are obviously far too perturbed by our company."

Without further word, she whisks Eulalie away, their tour beginning with the gallery and billiards room and ending upstairs, in a familiar stretch of hallway.

"This is my bedroom." She stops in front of the door. "Of course, you've already seen it."

"Show me again." Eulalie plays along. "Refresh my fading memory."

Her hands shaking and her palms clammy, Vera Mae fumbles the crystal door knob twice before getting a proper grip and managing to open it. Inside, she continues the charade of the tour, directing Eulalie around the room from one feature to another.

"Here you will find everything typical of a lady's bedroom: mirror, vanity, bed, coconut." She points to the latter on the bedside table. "Still unbreached."

"Not for very much longer if I have my way." Eulalie draws her over to the four-poster.

"Not here, Tigress," Vera Mae pleads weakly. "We mustn't do this here." She perches on the edge of the bed next to Eulalie. "You may have a kiss, but that is all." She lays her palm against Eulalie's cheek. "I do so want to taste your lips again."

"I want a good deal more than your lips." Eulalie grabs a pinch of Vera Mae's dress and eases it up, bunching it in her lap and laying a hand on her knee. "I want everything."

"Then take me somewhere." Vera Mae stays her hand, preventing her from going any higher. "Let's abscond."

"You want to flee your own party?"

"It's Reginald's party, and what I want is to do the most sinful things with you." Vera Mae guides Eulalie's hand up to the top of her stocking. "Today is the day." She lets Eulalie's fingertips graze her inner thigh. "No more waiting."

Eulalie mews like a hungry kitten. "But you won't give way here?"

"I dare not."

"Oh, God, give me strength." Eulalie sends her prayer up to the ceiling, then heaves herself off the bed, pulling Vera Mae with her. "I need you out of this house immediately. What's the quickest way?"

"The servants' stairwell. We must not be seen."

Without making a sound, they sneak from the bedroom into one of the narrow, darkened passages the servants use to move about the house like ghosts. Hand in hand, they steal down to the bowels of the building and emerge into the servants' quarters just in time to disrupt their supper, the sudden appearance of their mistress causing great consternation amongst the staff who all hurry to their feet as soon as Vera Mae enters the room.

"Begging your pardon." Vera Mae hurries through the servants' hall with Eulalie in tow. "Don't let us interrupt."

"Is everything all right, milady?" the butler asks.

"Yes, perfectly!" Vera Mae calls over her shoulder. "Miss Sauvage is taking very good care of me, and shall return me in due course." She flings open the back door and they spill out into the service alley running behind the house.

"We're free!" Eulalie picks her up and spins her around in circles.

"Oh, stop! Stop! Please! Mercy!" Vera Mae squeals, petitioning to be put down. "You'll make my head swim."

Eulalie sets her back on the ground.

"That's better." Vera Mae straightens her dress. "Now take me somewhere." She grabs Eulalie's lapels, pulls her close, and adopts a stern voice. "Don't make me ask you again. It's my birthday, and I want to be alone with you."

"Your birthday? Why did you not say?" Eulalie gives her rump a playful spank. "I've just aided and abetted you running out on your own birthday party."

"I told you: it's Reginald's party. I didn't ask for it." Vera Mae wraps her arms around Eulalie's neck. "There was only one person I cared to see."

"Still, you should've told me." Eulalie pouts. "I would've bought you a gift."

"I don't want a gift. Not one that comes from a shop anyway." Vera Mae urges Eulalie's hands onto her bum. "I am thirty years old this day, and I want this to be the most memorable birthday of my life."

"How can I make that happen for you?" Eulalie gives a sharp tug, mashing their bodies together. "What do you need?"

Vera Mae pinches her lower lip between her teeth, knowing that what she's about to say is very unladylike. "I have read in an unspeakably filthy book that there is an act one woman may perform upon another whereby she employs her mouth for the bringing of pleasure." Her cheeks burn. "Have you ever done such a thing?"

"God, yes." Eulalie brings her into a tighter embrace.

"Do you like it?"

Eulalie moves in, teasing her with the prospect of a kiss, hovering a mere hair's breadth away. "My mouth waters at the prospect."

"Would you do it to me?"

"Oh, my darling lady." Eulalie captures her lips in a kiss. "I will devour you."

"So whisk me away somewhere I cannot be found, and do so at once," Vera Mae implores her urgently. "Not your studio. Reginald knows of that place, and he may send someone after me when he discovers I'm missing."

"Don't worry." Eulalie beams. "I shall take you to the very last place anyone would ever think to look for you."

CHAPTER

VERA MAE PUSHES OPEN A HEAVY WOODEN DOOR AND STEPS inside a small, modest bedroom lit by an old oil lamp. She wouldn't exactly call it homey or cozy, but it will do. The furnishings are clean, albeit low-grade and well used, and the warped floorboards are covered with a threadbare rug. There's a tatty old sofa pushed against one wall, facing a double bed. A few towels have been laid out on one arm of the sofa, next to a small pot of cold cream, and there's a small washstand tucked into the corner of the room.

The bed itself is unsoiled and freshly made, but offers a minimal level of comfort. The sheets are thin, there's no counterpane, and the pillows look lumpy. No-one's meant to spend the night here, and if that weren't clue enough to the house's purpose, the sounds of a particular union between a man and a woman are emanating from the room next door.

"This isn't quite what you would call a hotel is it?" Vera Mae finds a complimentary rubber condom on the washstand, next to a vaginal douching syringe.

"Not quite." Eulalie locks the door behind them. "But it suits our needs."

Vera Mae grins. "Have you brought me to a house of assignation?"

She doesn't need Eulalie to answer that. Excited by the prospect of something so outrageously indecent, she claps her hands together gleefully.

"I've heard of such places, but I never imagined even for a moment that I'd ever see inside one." She looks around, exploring everything.

"I hope you won't mind it too much." Eulalie gives the bed a close inspection, making sure it's fit enough for a baroness. "I couldn't very well take you to Claridge's. For one thing, it's a little out of my financial capabilities. For another, I'm quite sure a woman such as yourself can't be seen within a mile of a proper hotel bedroom without scrutiny and scandal."

"I hardly think it could hurt." Vera Mae chuckles. "I am already the subject of so much gossip on account of my association with you."

"Does that bother you?"

"I won't let it." Vera Mae slips Eulalie's jacket off her shoulders, keen to unrig her. "I have made a promise to myself—and also to you—that I will no longer deny what I feel. Nor will I be ashamed of it. So when people see us together on the street, I will not let go of your arm. When those around me suggest that there is anything wrong in how we are, I will not apologize."

As she folds Eulalie's jacket and lays it neatly on the sofa, something in the wall catches her eye. It's a hole. Bored through a natural knot occurring in a vertical wooden support beam, it's usually covered by a cheap painting, but vibrations from the vigorous activity next door have caused the artwork to shift.

"What in the world ... ?" Vera Mae clambers up onto the sofa and puts her eye to the hole, peering through to the room on the other side. Realizing what it is, she recoils, slaps a hand over her mouth, and stifles a guffaw.

"You will not believe this, but there is a peephole in this wall!" She peeks again. "Furthermore, there is a viscount in that room defiling a woman in the most abject and merciless way, and she is certainly not his wife."

Eulalie climbs up beside her and has a gander. "I can definitely vouch for that." She tries not to laugh too loudly. "That woman is no lady."

"You recognize her?" Vera Mae infers. "Is she one of your whores? Ought I be envious?"

"I painted her." Eulalie has one more look.

"That is all?" Vera Mae fishes for reassurance.

"That is all, I promise." Eulalie hops down onto the floor. "I certainly did not do to her what I am about to do to you." She scoops Vera Mae off the sofa and carries her to the bed, laying her softly upon it. "Are you ready?"

"My darling tigress." Vera Mae props herself up on her elbows, watching Eulalie doff her waistcoat and tie. "I'm so ready for you."

Eulalie crawls onto the bed and begins at Vera Mae's feet, kissing her ankles, her shins, and her knees. She takes her time. As her kisses move northward, so her hands glide up Vera Mae's long, shapely legs, raising her dress till it crumples around her hips.

"You're so beautiful." She parts Vera Mae's thighs and kneels between them. "I love seeing you this way." She crooks Vera Mae's knees to the ceiling, positioning her for the receiving of pleasure. "I swear there is no sight more erotic than a genteel woman offering up the delights of her sex, and I cherish this moment all the more for knowing that, after all these years of deprivation, it is me you've chosen to share yourself with."

She lies atop Vera Mae, crushing their breasts together. "You've waited so long." She hugs Vera Mae's thighs around her hips. "Your untouched sex must be aching to reach the sweet pinnacle of desire."

Vera Mae whines, her sodden knickers clinging to her core, the saturated silk tickling her throbbing flesh. "I have such an impatience in me. The very thought of your touch has me on the threshold of ecstasy."

"I want you." Eulalie dives between her thighs. "Every bit of you."

Vera Mae closes her eyes and holds her breath, waiting for her knickers to be wrenched away, but ... nothing happens. Seconds pass and Eulalie's hands grubble around under her dress, as if confused, seeking an elusive entry point.

"What are you doing down there?" she asks after a while, wondering what all the fumbling is about. "The fastening is at the back." She lifts her bum, trying to help.

"Underneath how many layers of silk and frou frou?" Eulalie grumbles, her access impeded by the knee-length directoire knickers, which in turn are trapped beneath the garters attached to Vera Mae's corset.

"Try the buttons then." Vera Mae directs her to the buttons running down the right hip of the garment, so designed for the ease of tending to bathroom needs.

"Your knickers are ridiculous." Eulalie growls with frustration. "How is a woman to invite pleasure while wearing a pair of these?"

"She is not." Vera Mae giggles. "That is the point of them: to deter such doings."

"Well, to hell with them." Eulalie takes hold of the knickers and tears them open at the crotch, right along the seam.

"Oh!" Vera Mae shrieks. "You have shredded my under things!" She sits up and inspects the damage, more amused by Eulalie's undisciplined fervor than she is annoyed by the destruction of her knickers. "How am I to explain that to my maid?!"

"Those of us who routinely dress and undress ourselves unaided have little sympathy for that particular predicament, milady." Eulalie winks.

"Milady!" Vera Mae snorts. "I do not feel very much like a lady at this moment. Nor, I daresay, do I look like one." She returns to her recumbent pose, wishing there was a mirror so that she could see herself. "I expect I look despicably wanton."

"Breathtakingly wanton," Eulalie concurs, holding her knickers open, admiring her weeping sex, her flushed pink labia glistening with arousal, her hardened clit swollen with lust. "In fact, you're the most perfect woman I've ever seen." She drops a kiss on the dense, lush thicket of dark auburn hair on Vera Mae's mound and breathes deep, inhaling the intoxicating aroma of her womanhood. "So, so perfect."

Her next kiss lands directly on the protruding nub at the apex of Vera Mae's lubricious slit, and Vera Mae wails. Another kiss produces the same reaction. And another. One more. She then alternates her attentions between that critical spot and the plump, soft, furrow below, teasing, licking, and sucking, devoting every energy to the work.

Unable to restrain herself, Vera Mae pants and groans and howls all the way through Eulalie's oral ministrations till her thighs begin to quiver.

"I think it's happening," she whispers breathlessly, an exquisite pressure building within her. "My God, I think I'm at my peak!" She clamps her hands on the back of Eulalie's head, gripping her blonde mane. "Oh, I truly am!" She cries out, her sex in spasms. "I love you! My darling, I love you!"

When the sensations ebb away, she untwists her fingers from Eulalie's hair. "You are magnificent." She writhes on the bed, relishing every last contraction. "Is it always so intense? It is impossible to use one's indoor voice while under such an assault."

"That's how you know I'm doing it right." Eulalie flops down beside her. "Did you mean what you said when you were in the grip of it? Do you love me? Or were you merely overcome with passion?"

"I love you, Tigress." Vera Mae snuggles up to her chest. "And I want you to know that I've made an appointment to see my brother."

"Your brother?" Eulalie wraps her up in an embrace. "What for?"

"He inherited our father's title." Vera Mae traces a finger around one of Eulalie's aroused nipples, teasing it over her cotton shirt. "He is the current earl, and therefore is the one in charge of our family's estate." She unbuttons the shirt and slips her hand inside. "I must make arrangements to leave Regent's Park."

Eulalie rolls them both over, smiling down on her. "This is truly what you want?"

"To be with you? Yes." Vera Mae grabs her shirt and pulls her into a kiss. "Not for a few stolen moments in a house of ill repute, but properly. I want to share more than just a bed with you." She keeps Eulalie held close. "Tell me you feel the same."

"I do." Eulalie reengages her lips and navigates a hand up her dress, driving through the split in her knickers and caressing her sex. "I love you, Vera." She dips a single digit into Vera Mae's treasure, breaching the gateway to her body. "I love you so much."

Vera Mae gasps as Eulalie enters her. "Say it again."

"I *love* you." Eulalie eases another finger inside her, stretching her open.

"Be gentle." Vera Mae groans, clutching a fistful of the bed sheets. "Do be gentle."

Taking care not to cause her any discomfort, Eulalie strokes every ridge and groove, probing the very deepest parts of her tight channel until she brings on another divine climax, this one erupting with more certainty.

"Yes, yes, yes!" Vera Mae feels her orgasm about to crest. "That's it!" She throws her head back and moans, her body rigid, trembling, then limp, the crisis passed.

She would be happy to lie there for the rest of the night, safe in Eulalie's arms, but it gets late, their time in the room expires, and Eulalie walks her home, bidding her goodnight at the servants' entrance they bolted from hours earlier.

"Thank you for indulging me today." Vera Mae makes the most of her last few moments with Eulalie. "It has been a birthday I will never forget." She encourages Eulalie's arms around her waist. "You have given me my first taste of true pleasure."

She makes a bid for Eulalie's lips, but as they come together, Bennett appears from the back door, tiptoeing out to have a cigarette before retiring to bed.

"I do apologize, milady." She staggers backwards, shocked to catch her mistress in a clinch. "I didn't see nothing of anything." She spins around to face the wall and stands like a statue, pretending to be invisible—as is the customary response for any servant when accidentally coming upon one of their employers in the house.

"Not a word to His Lordship about this," Vera Mae warns her, making no attempt to separate herself from Eulalie. "I daresay I'm in enough trouble with him already."

"He's not been best pleased this evening, milady." Bennett keeps her eyes averted.

"What has he said?"

Bennett remains silent, staring at the ground.

"Oh, come on, Bennett," Vera Mae urges her. "I care not what the man thinks of me."

Bennett swallows hard before answering. "He said you've become delirious with grief and not been acting quite like yourself." She hesitates to say more. "He wonders if another stay at Burley House might do you some good."

"Ha! Not on his life!" Vera Mae clings tighter to Eulalie. "I am quite within my own mind and not in the least bit upset, I can assure you."

"What's Burley House?" Eulalie raises a questioning eyebrow.

"No place I ever intend to go back to." Vera Mae buries her face against Eulalie's shoulder. "It's a private nursing home for women with nervous disorder, and I spent a spell there last year, after ... well, when I was at my lowest ebb." She pushes aside the unwanted memories and helps herself to Eulalie's lips once more. "I must go." She pries herself away. "Goodnight, Tigress. You make me so very happy." She turns to Bennett. "Escort me up the quiet way. I do not wish His Lordship to see me returning."

"As you wish, milady." Bennett leads her back to her bedroom via the servants' passages and prepares to disrobe her for bed, but is swiftly dismissed.

"That'll be all for tonight." Vera Mae sends the confused maid off without explanation, suddenly remembering that her knickers are in a despicable state on account of Eulalie's exuberance. "Thank you for your discretion. I know you don't approve."

"I don't want to see you hurt, milady. That's the sum of it." Bennett performs a quick curtsey, still unable to look her mistress in the eye. "Goodnight now." She tiptoes away with practiced stealth.

Once alone, Vera Mae casts her clothes off onto the floor, leaving them for Bennett to clear away in the morning, and inspects her torn knickers with a satisfied smile before secreting them inside her pillowcase until an opportunity for permanent disposal presents itself.

CHAPTER

Friday June 27, 1913

VERA MAE STIRS ANOTHER SPOONFUL OF HONEY INTO HER tea, waiting for her brother's response to her news, fully expecting him to be displeased with her—as he always has been. This is the first time she's visited her family's Oxfordshire estate since her marriage, and everything on home turf is just as awkward as she remembers. No matter how many years pass, being here always makes her feel like a little girl. A disobedient little girl.

"For goodness sake, say something, William." She prompts her brother out of his silence. "Or are we to sit here gawping at each other all afternoon?"

"What is there to say? You have made your decision." William straightens his thick mustache and sighs, his disappointment evident. "You will not marry Reginald."

"I cannot." Vera Mae gazes across the lawn on which she played as a child, glad that they opted to take tea outside rather than in the stuffy old house, every room suffused with unpleasant memories. "I do not love him."

"Is there someone else?"

"It's complicated." She watches her young nieces and nephews chase a good-natured Labrador back and forth, teasing him with a ball, unable to remember a moment in her own childhood when she was that carefree. "I cannot say that you will be pleased."

"Oh, God, is he a Jew?" William glowers at her across the small garden table, prepared for a fight. "Don't tell me you've gone and fallen for a bloody Jew?"

"Not a Jew." Vera Mae anticipates an even worse reaction to the truth. "Nor a man."

On account of the proximity of the children, William stifles his worst objections into a series of half-mumbled expletives. "I thought we were over all this nonsense, Vera."

"I have tried." Vera Mae keeps her voice appropriately hushed. "I have done things your way my whole life. I have pleased you and our father, now he and my husband are in the grave, and I wish to please myself. Is that so wrong?"

"You will be a disgrace."

Those words no longer hurt her. "I have always been a disgrace to this family, William."

She recalls being caught cuddling one of the housemaids when she was thirteen. An act which resulted in the maid's immediate dismissal without a character and her rapid enrollment in a finishing school far, far away. Out of sight, out of mind.

"Nevertheless, I have done all that was asked of me, despite my feelings." Vera Mae suppresses her childhood trauma. "I married the man our father chose for me, and never once did I utter a single word of a complaint. I was a good and faithful wife."

"What has changed in you?"

"I have met the most beautiful and tender woman." Vera Mae smiles at the thought of Eulalie. "She's a—"

"Spare me the details of your vulgarity." William cringes.

"What is vulgar about it, William? It is love, that is all."

"Love?" He grimaces. "You love this woman?" The concept is as unfathomable to him as a man marrying a goat.

"Yes, I *love* her." Vera Mae clasps a hand over her heart. "So deeply you cannot even begin to imagine."

"I do not *want* to imagine."

Vera Mae's face falls. "Do you not want to see me happy, William? Is there no compassion in you at all?"

"I cannot condone this." William denies her his blessing. "But you are my sister. I will not see you ruined, nor cast out onto the street. I owe it to our parents to see that you are kept comfortable, though I must warn you: if you insist upon this course of life, this is all I will do for you. There will be no more. Affairs between us will be settled." He consults his pocket watch, signaling the conclusion of their business. "I must protect the family. I'm sure you understand."

"Perfectly." Vera Mae gets the hint.

"Does Reginald know what you're planning?"

"Not yet." She finishes her tea and stands up, dusting biscuit crumbs off her skirt. "Please do not breathe a word of this to him. I will tell him as soon as my arrangements have been made."

She shows herself out.

Vera Mae's spirits are buoyed the moment she returns to Regent's Park and discovers there is a package waiting for her from Eulalie. She finds it on the foot of her bed: a delicate box bound with satin ribbons. Not large enough to be a hat or a dress, she suspects it might be a scarf, a pair of gloves, or perhaps even stockings. A belated birthday present?

With all the glee of a child on Christmas morning, she unfurls the ribbons and opens the box, revealing a pair of silk French knickers. Lingerie! Much shorter and lacier than the comparatively modest directoire knickers she usually wears, they look positively indecent. With them is an elegant, handwritten note:

Out with the old, in with the new.
Dinner is booked for 7 o'clock.

She can't help herself. She throws off her clothes and puts the knickers on immediately, standing before the cheval mirror to admire them, loving how they hug her buttocks and leave her thighs bared above her stockings.

"You're a wicked woman, Vera Mae," she tells her blushing reflection. "You look like such a tart." Turning to the side, she runs her hands over her bum, evaluating her new appearance from all angles. "And you are enjoying it ever so much."

Not wanting Bennett to see her in these new, far more daring undergarments, she dresses herself for her date with Eulalie, layering her best dress on top of her best corset, on top of her best chemise. As it nears seven o'clock, she dons her hat, gloves, and jacket, and instructs the chauffeur to pull the motorcar up outside.

"Where do you think you're going?" Reginald questions her on the doorstep.

"I'm having dinner with some friends." She steps into the waiting motorcar as the chauffeur holds the door open for her. "Don't wait up late on my account."

Truthfully, she expects to be back at the Regent's Park house before midnight, but much to her delight, the date doesn't end with dinner. After the restaurant, Eulalie takes her to a cabaret and theater club on Heddon Street: a small, nondescript cul-de-sac off Regent Street. Located in the basement of a draper's warehouse, the club doesn't look like much from the exterior, and Vera Mae regards it with some suspicion.

"Where in the world are you leading me, Tigress?"

Eulalie guides her down a flight of steps to the club entrance below the level of the pavement, where a large sign decorated with a yellow cow proclaims the name of the establishment: The Cave of the Golden Calf.

Inside, the dingy basement has been converted into a thriving club. Chairs and tables surround a small stage for live musical performances, readings of poetry, or other artistic fare, and the walls are decorated with futurist-inspired murals, stars painted on the low ceiling.

"Whatever is this place?" Vera Mae looks around, seeing a pleasantly surprising mix of the wealthy, the aristocratic, and the bohemian, men with men, women with women, and men and women together. No segregation, and no prejudice.

Eulalie explains that it's a place for artists and intellectuals to mingle with one another. Regular patrons include the Lady Diana Manners—supposedly the most attractive woman in all of England—Raymond Asquith, the Prime Minister's son, and a whole array of writers, actors, and poets.

For Vera Mae, the atmosphere is thrilling. It's a place free of judgment. A place they can drink and dance and flirt without ever a questioning look or a disgusted glare being cast their way. A place where women may converse on any topic without fear of mockery or reprimand. A place of complete acceptance.

She's in no hurry to leave, but Eulalie eventually coaxes her back to the studio with the promise of intimate pleasures.

Once there, Vera Mae takes the lead, drawing Eulalie by the hand into the room beyond the curtain. At the bedside, she eases Eulalie's jacket off her shoulders and lets it fall to the floor. She unbuttons her waistcoat next, giving it the same treatment. Then her tie. Her shirt ...

Vera Mae cups her trembling hands around Eulalie's denuded breasts, pinching and teasing both nipples between her fingers, exciting them to full rigidity. "They're so responsive to touch." She rubs them against her palms. "Is the same true of all your parts, I wonder?"

She trails her hands down to Eulalie's waist, intending to find out, but before she reaches the fastening of Eulalie's trousers, she's distracted by an old scar she didn't catch sight of the first time she saw Eulalie topless. It begins at Eulalie's right hip and extends some way over her back.

"However did you get this?" She turns Eulalie around to get a better look at it. "A dog whip?" she guesses, judging by the appearance of it. "Your parents?"

"The police." Eulalie lets her inspect it. "November 18, 1910."

Vera Mae remembers the date: Black Friday. On that day, three hundred suffragettes marched to parliament to protest the abandonment of the first conciliation bill— some armed with hammers and bags of stones for the purpose of breaking windows. There was much violence. The police lashed out, giving the women beatings and worse, and over a hundred suffragettes were arrested during the six-hour onslaught.

"I got away relatively unscathed and left for France soon after." Eulalie runs her fingers over the scar. "It could've been worse. My mother was among those imprisoned."

Vera Mae kneels on the bed and draws Eulalie close, laying kisses on the scar, then her stomach, her ribs, and more. For the first time, she wraps her lips around one of Eulalie's nipples and sucks the firm bud into her mouth.

"It feels so good to touch you," she mewls, urging Eulalie onto the bed with her.

Lying down, they fold into each other's arms, their lips locked together, their limbs entwined. Then something concealed in Eulalie's trousers jabs Vera Mae's crotch.

"Whatever is this thing in your pocket?" She reaches for it, wrapping her hand around a strangely phallic object strapped to Eulalie's thigh. "It's poking me."

Eulalie colors up. "It's a replica of the male instrument." She encourages Vera Mae to examine the shape of it. "I wear it sometimes."

"For what purpose?"

"I like the way it makes me feel." She moves Vera Mae's hand up and down the shaft. "Especially when I'm using it upon a woman."

"I've never heard of such a thing." Vera Mae looks baffled. "May I see it?"

As requested, Eulalie unfastens her trousers, releases the phallus from her thigh, and lets it spring up from her groin: eight inches of perfectly molded glass.

"You would put this inside me?" Vera Mae takes hold of it again.

"If you would let me." Eulalie watches her massage it. "Oh, God, if you would let me."

Vera Mae shuffles down to study it at close range, intrigued by the possibility. "If I'm quite honest, it was not exactly the sensations of my husband's exertions that I found displeasing. My disappointment with the operation lay almost entirely in the repulsively masculine form to which the instrument was always unavoidably attached." She circles a finger around the mushroom-shaped tip of Eulalie's cock. "Do you ever wish it could do all of a man's work?"

"Frequently." Eulalie flips Vera Mae onto her back, bunches up her dress, rolls on top of her, and assumes the appropriate position, grinding the dildo against her sex. "I would get you in so much trouble."

The notion of that ought to be funny, but Vera Mae finds no humor in it. Instead, the mere thought of being with child triggers a pained sob.

"Oh, if only you could!" She buries her face against Eulalie's chest and weeps, one hand pressed to her aching belly. "I would give anything ..."

"I'm sorry." Eulalie consoles her. "I had no idea you wanted a babe."

Vera Mae pulls a hanky from her pocket and stems the flow of tears. "Over the last year, I have had some very great difficulty coming to terms with the fact that I will never be a mother ... that I cannot bring myself to do what it takes to become a mother." She sniffles. "I thought, in time, I would resign myself to accept Reginald for the business." She gazes up at Eulalie, smiling weakly. "Then I met you. My savior."

"You know, a woman does not have to bear a child to be a mother." Eulalie kisses away her tears. "There are plenty children in this world who would benefit from—"

"Hush." Vera Mae silences her. "No more of this tonight." She puts her arms around Eulalie and pulls her into a hug. "Just hold me."

As their bodies press together, Eulalie's cock makes a bid for entry into Vera Mae's body, the hard tip grazing her clit and lodging in the valley of her sex, only the silk French knickers barring its way.

Vera Mae moans and slides her hands onto Eulalie's rump, preventing her from pulling away. "Do that again."

Eager to please, Eulalie adjusts her priapic appendage so that it nestles snugly against Vera Mae's critical parts and thrusts rhythmically, generating the most delicious friction.

"You're making me want it." Vera Mae meets every thrust with a sympathetic wiggle of her bum. "Do it to me now."

Eulalie drives a hand up her dress, ready to do battle with the directoire knickers, and breaks into a grin when she feels the French knickers instead. "You're wearing them."

"Such a wicked gift." Vera Mae giggles. "They're utterly obscene!"

Eulalie grabs a fistful of them, preparing to tug them down, but freezes at the sound of someone knocking sharply on the door to her studio.

Silence.

More frantic knocking.

"Milady, please answer. His Lordship knows you're here, and I've been sent for you."

Vera Mae recognizes Bennett's voice calling to her. Angered by the interruption, she wriggles out from under Eulalie and answers the door.

"What is the meaning of this? Has His Lordship mistaken himself for my keeper?"

"He wishes for you to come home directly." Bennett keeps her head dipped, shying from her mistress's wrath.

"He says he has a matter of some urgency to discuss with you."

"At this time of night?"

"Don't go." Eulalie approaches, her shirt hastily buttoned and everything tucked away, the dildo creating a prominent bulge in her crotch, making it appear as though she is in possession of a virile member in full tumescence. "Stay here with me. You're a free woman. You need not jump at his command."

Bennett gawks at her apparent erection.

"I've never been free." Vera Mae sighs. "But that will soon change." She instructs Bennett to wait for her outside and talks to Eulalie alone. "I saw my brother today, and have begun making arrangements to leave Regent's Park—just as I said I would."

"And?" Eulalie seizes her by the waist.

"And ... he may have betrayed me to Reginald. I can't think what else His Lordship would cause this much fuss over." Vera Mae lays her hand over Eulalie's dildo, rubbing it through her trousers. "Have a little more patience, Tigress. I will be yours, I promise you, but I am not yet at liberty to do entirely as I please. I must be careful."

She pacifies Eulalie with a kiss, then returns to Regent's Park, finding Reginald in his study and primed for a fight.

"You lied to me," he snarls at her over a glass of whiskey. "You've been out with that damn suffragette artist again."

"Are you having me followed?" Vera Mae folds her arms defensively. "Miss Sauvage and I had dinner together, not that it's any of your concern. I was thanking her for her excellent work. The portrait is finished."

"She was paid. Was that not thanks enough?" Reginald sets down his glass and rummages in one of his desk drawers. "I was hoping it wouldn't come to this, but you've given me no choice." He pulls out a file full of papers. "I know all about your little invert."

Vera Mae spots the motif of a private investigation firm on the corner of the file. "You have had her investigated?! How dare you! What right do you have to meddle in my personal affairs?"

"It is for your own good, you'll see." He takes another sip of his whiskey and opens the file. "Her name is not Eulalie Sauvage. Did you know that? Her real name is Olivia Meux."

"What of it?" Vera Mae shrugs. "Many artists use different, more exotic names. It certainly isn't unusual. She picked up the name Sauvage while she was studying in Paris."

"How about her husband?" Reginald forges on. "Did she tell you about him?"

A chill runs down Vera Mae's spine, her silence speaking volumes.

"It appears she has absconded from him," Reginald goes on. "I have the name of the man here, along with his address and place of employment." He flicks through the papers. "Nasty piece of work he is, too. The man is a thug with convictions for battery and assault. Fancies himself a bit of a boxer. Now what do you suppose he might do if he learned the whereabouts of his estranged wife? Do you think he might go after her?"

Vera Mae remains silent, tears welling in her eyes and tumbling down her cheeks.

"Listen carefully to me, Vera." Reginald closes the file. "I don't want to hurt you. You've had your fun. Now if you care anything for this woman, you will put this nonsense aside. Surely you would not wish to see her returned to the life she fled?"

"I will not marry you." Vera Mae clenches her fists, her hands shaking with anger. "No matter what you do, I will *not* be your wife."

"Yes, you will." Reginald locks the file away. "Because without me, you have nothing." He finishes his drink. "Be a good girl now. Don't do anything foolish."

Dismissed, Vera Mae retreats to her bedroom, falls upon the bed, and cries herself to sleep.

CHAPTER

Saturday July 5, 1913

VERA MAE LIES IN BED, EULALIE'S COCONUT BESIDE HER ON the pillow. She's been exchanging letters with Eulalie since the night they last saw one another, sending and receiving them through Bennett so as not to draw Reginald's attention, but even twice daily correspondence barely takes the edge off the pain of being kept from her.

In each letter, Eulalie pleads to know what's wrong, but Vera Mae insists they must wait for an opportunity to discuss everything face to face. The matter is too sensitive. Too delicate. Too complicated. Much too complicated.

Frustrated, and wound up to an unbearable pitch, Vera Mae dips a hand beneath the counterpane, slips inside her French knickers, and touches herself, trying to replicate the sensations of Eulalie's expert titillation ... but it's not the same. After a few fruitless minutes, she gives up and screams into her pillow. A moment later, Bennett arrives.

"Is he gone? Vera Mae sits bolt upright, hopeful.

Bennett nods. "He just left, milady."

"Finally!" Vera Mae flings back the counterpane and leaps out of bed.

She's been waiting for Reginald to leave on business so that she might sneak out of the house unnoticed, and now is the time. She dresses quickly and simply—skirt, blouse, hat, gloves—and hurries to the studio with a silk motoring scarf pulled over her head to help obscure her identity, looking over her shoulder every five seconds to make sure she's not being followed.

When she gets to the studio, her unexpected arrival cuts short a risqué photography session involving several naked prostitutes, a number of large feathers, a bit of hot wax, and some particularly creative uses for silk rope.

After a passionate greeting, Eulalie sends them all away, pours Vera Mae a glass of brandy, and seats her on the sofa. "I've missed you so much." She kneels at Vera Mae's feet. "I cannot suffer this separation a moment longer." She rucks Vera Mae's skirt up in her lap and caresses her calves, dropping kisses on her stockinged knees and thighs. "What has happened to keep you from me? Is it your brother? Did he betray you to Reginald?"

"No, my brother has kept his word. The trouble is that Reginald has had you investigated." Vera Mae sips the brandy for courage. "He says your name is Olivia Meux, and that you are married. Is it true?"

The kisses stop.

"I haven't been that woman in a long time." Eulalie gets up from the floor, all trace of happiness erased from her expression. "Nor do I wish to be again." She pours herself a glass of brandy. "What threat has Reginald made? I presume he is using this as leverage."

"If I do not sever my relationship with you, he will inform your husband of your new life here in London." Vera Mae downs the rest of the brandy and holds the glass out for a refill, sensing she'll be in need of it. "He will ruin you."

Eulalie knocks back her own drink and pours them each another. "Does he know my husband is a heartless brute who communicates only with his fists and prick?"

"He has seen the convictions, yes." Vera Mae welcomes more booze. "Why did you ever marry such a man?"

"The choice was not mine to make." Eulalie demolishes her second helping of brandy. "I was nineteen years old, and it was my father's will, not my own. He thought marriage would cure me of my irregularities. I had no say in the matter."

"I understand that perfectly." Vera Mae empties her own glass and sets it aside. "But why did you not petition for a divorce? Surely his cruelty would've been grounds enough?"

"I hadn't the money." Eulalie laments her predicament. "The last time he did his worst on me, I had him convicted of aggravated assault and obtained a protection order. It was the best I could do. Ironically, the police who came to arrest him were the very same men who delivered me to my last beating."

"Delivered you?" Vera Mae urges her to sit. "Delivered you how?"

"They picked me up at a suffrage protest that turned violent." Eulalie slumps onto the sofa. "Rather than lock me up in Holloway Prison, they thought justice would be best served by taking me home so that I might be taught a lesson by my husband instead."

Vera Mae's heart aches for her. "But the protection order worked, yes?" She wants that to be true. "He never hurt you again?"

Eulalie shakes her head. "He refused to relinquish his hold on me. That's why I reverted to my maiden name—Chase—and fled to the continent. While I was there, I became Eulalie Sauvage."

"Well, why not file for a divorce now?" Vera Mae clings to the only fragment of hope she can find in the situation. "Let me help. If you still lack the funds, I can—"

"No." Eulalie shuts her down. "I cannot divorce him now. If I begin legal proceedings of any sort against him, he will find out that I ..." She lets her words trail off.

"Find out what?" Vera Mae clasps their hands together. "Whatever the trouble is, we can surmount it. We shall hire the very best lawyers, and—"

"I have a child." Eulalie knocks her for six.

Scarcely able to breathe, Vera Mae manages to whisper: "His?"

"I've been with no other man." Eulalie backhands a tear from her eye. "I became aware of my condition not long after the protection order was granted, when I was hospitalized for this." She lays a hand over the scar she acquired on Black Friday. "I couldn't bear for him to know—I feared what he might do—so Olivia Meux disappeared. She had to."

"Are you afraid of losing custody?"

Eulalie nods. "He would take her from me just to spite me."

"But how could he?" Vera Mae frowns. "He is a violent brute. You are her mother, and you are of excellent character."

"Am I?" Eulalie raises a doubtful eyebrow. "By whose standards? Even if my past with the WSPU did not count against me—which it most definitely does—and even if mothers had the same parental rights as men— which we do not—I have never made any secret of my irregular proclivities. Not even in marriage. When I was newly wedded, I conspired to be with women in any way I could, which often meant inviting my amours into the bed I shared with my husband—a sport he rather encouraged."

"But there is no evidence of this?" Vera Mae tries to remain positive. "It will be the word of a confirmed wife beater over your own."

"Sadly, there is evidence of the best sort." Eulalie sighs. "He has in his possession some compromising photographic images. Photographs in which I am exuberantly expressing my very great love of the female form."

"They are pornographic?"

"They would have me condemned a deviant whore." Eulalie dries her eyes on her sleeve. "If he was of a mind to, which I'm certain he would be, he could take my little girl from me. I would lose her."

"Why did you ever come back here?" Vera Mae bites back her own tears. "Why did you not stay in Paris, where you were both safe?"

"My mother was taken ill," Eulalie reminds her of the fact. "Since her stroke, she's been unable to work. She fell behind on her rent and faced eviction from our London home."

"You returned to help her." Vera Mae sympathizes. "And what of your daughter?"

"Flora stays with her at a cottage I rent for them in Kent. I send money every week and visit as often as I can." Eulalie pulls a small photograph of a smiling toddler with perfect blonde curls out of her pocket and shows it to Vera Mae. "I was going to tell you about her when you confided in me that you wanted a child."

Vera Mae admires the picture. "But what use could I be to her? She already has a loving mother."

"Who says she can't have two?" Eulalie replaces the photograph in her pocket. "All children want and need is to be loved and cared for. Whether they have a mother and father, two mothers, or two fathers, it matters not in the end." She lays a hand on Vera Mae's knee. "So where does this leave us? Are we doomed? Or is there a way? Does Reginald know about Flora?"

"I don't think so." Vera Mae sinks her head onto Eulalie's shoulder, pained by the impossibility of their situation. "And I cannot abide the thought of putting you at risk of discovery."

Eulalie begins to withdraw.

"But"—Vera Mae clamps Eulalie's hand in place on her knee—"I cannot quit you, Tigress. My heart will not allow it." She parts her thighs an inch, inviting Eulalie to explore the more intimate regions to be found north of her stockings.

"So what must we do?" Eulalie accepts the invitation. "Any ideas?"

"Not even the first." Vera Mae welcomes Eulalie's hand inside her French knickers. "For now, if we are to keep seeing one another, it must be done on the hush."

"Are we safe at this moment?" Eulalie teases her throbbing sex till it's slick with need.

"Yes." Vera Mae's thighs tremble. "His Lordship is away for the day."

"Then come to bed and let me have you properly." Eulalie disengages, gets up, and wanders into the bedroom, leaving her teetering on the brink of pleasure.

Lightheaded and half delirious, Vera Mae sheds her hat, gloves, and scarf, heaves herself off the sofa, and follows a trail of Eulalie's discarded clothing to the bed. There, Eulalie awaits her naked, lying atop the counterpane, her head propped on the heel of her palm.

"Take off your clothes," she instructs, smiling. "I'll watch."

"I'm afraid I don't know how to make a show of it." Vera Mae peels off her blouse and camisole. "Not like those beautiful young women in the burlesque halls." She wriggles out of her skirt. "I've never tried to be alluring."

"You don't have to try." Eulalie enjoys the view. "You are so naturally."

"Flatterer." Vera Mae props one foot on the edge of the bed and unclips her garter straps, then does the other. "I'm sure you say that to all your women."

"Only the baronesses." Eulalie winks. "Now remove your knickers."

Giggling, Vera Mae eases down her knickers and tosses them at Eulalie's face. They hit their target, and Eulalie holds them to her nose, inhaling deeply.

"God, you smell like a woman who needs a fuck."

Vera Mae gawps in astonishment, having never before heard Eulalie use such coarse language. "Is that supposed to be a compliment?"

"Absolutely." Eulalie flings the knickers aside. "Your sex is ripe, and that's very, very arousing."

"That's not all you're hungry for, though, is it?" Vera Mae unhooks her corset and tears it away. "You must surely want these." She cups her chemise-covered breasts. "They're big, aren't they?" She squeezes her hands around them as best she can, but they don't fit neatly in her palms the way Eulalie's do. "Heavy, too." She releases them, letting them jiggle and bounce. "Hard to confine them in a corset all day."

Eulalie groans. "Show me."

At her urging, Vera Mae pulls off her chemise, baring her ample charms.

"Oh, Vera ..." Eulalie pulls her onto the bed. "You're the most divine woman I've ever laid my eyes on."

"Touch me." Vera Mae snatches up Eulalie's hands and brings them to her bosom. "I want to be touched. I want you all over me."

Eulalie lies her down, caressing her firm, full breasts.

"More," Vera Mae begs. "Kiss them."

Eulalie repositions between her thighs and drops kisses all over her soft belly, then higher. She engulfs one nipple in her mouth, pinching it lightly between her teeth, biting, tugging, and sucking, and teases the other between her fingers.

"They're so sensitive." Vera Mae urges her to suckle. "I could almost come."

"You will." Eulalie crushes their bodies together, pinning her to the counterpane, their parts aligned from loins to bust. "We'll come as one. Your pleasure will bring mine on." She rocks her hips forward, grinding against Vera Mae. Slowly at first, then fast.

Yowling on every thrust, Vera Mae grips Eulalie's buttocks. She's never felt anything so intense. Skin against skin. Their bodies so closely entwined. Such intimacy! As her orgasm erupts, her sex racked with convulsions, Eulalie's rhythm breaks above her. They become a bundle of twitching limbs, their climaxes peaking in unison, their wails of shared ecstasy muffled by their frantic, amorous kisses.

As the moment of crisis ebbs away, Eulalie collapses on the bed beside her, panting heavily. "Christ almighty, that felt good."

All Vera Mae can do is whimper. While she lies there, recovering her capacity for language, she catches her reflection in a mirror leaning against the wall on the far side of the room and contemplates her nudity.

"Do you realize that, until today, I'd never taken my clothes off in front of anyone but my maid? Isn't that frightfully silly?" She takes one of her breasts in her hand. "No-one else has ever seen me this way, let alone felt my charms."

"Your husband never ... ?"

Vera Mae snorts. "My husband believed the only purpose of a woman's bosom was to nourish an infant. He found no amusement in them." She tweaks one of her nipples. "Do yours ever ache? Since you had your child, do they react to the presence of a baby as if it were your own? As if they might produce milk at any moment."

"Not since Flora weaned." Eulalie casts her mind back. "But while she was still on my breast, I had only to hear the cry of a babe—any babe—and my nipples would weep. What makes you ask?" She rolls to face Vera Mae, her brow creased with confusion. "Surely only a woman who's borne a child of her own could think of such a thing."

Vera Mae turns her face into the pillow and weeps.

"Vera ..." Eulalie peppers her head with kisses. "Tell me."

"I was with child," Vera Mae gets out between sobs. "When my husband and I boarded that godforsaken ship to America last year, my belly was full. I had not long left before my confinement. He was heavy in me."

"What happened?" Eulalie asks in a quiet voice.

"I was one of the first into the lifeboats. Women in my condition and of my class got precedence." She clamps a hand over her stomach. "I felt the pains as they lowered us into the water. It was too soon, but he was determined to make his entrance into the world. And there was blood. Lots of blood. I knew something was wrong." She pauses to steady her breathing.

"By the time we were rescued by the Carpathia, he'd stopped moving." She swallows hard. "I never felt him move again. He died inside me, but the pains did not stop." She seeks solace against Eulalie's chest. "I bore a child who never took a breath. It's *his* death I've been mourning this past year, not my husband's."

"I'm so sorry." Eulalie lifts up her head and kisses her damp face, tears of sympathy tumbling down her own cheeks. "No woman should ever have to suffer as you have."

"That is why we must find a way to fix this dreadful mess with your husband and Reginald." Vera Mae summons strength. "I lost a child. You will *not* be made to lose yours."

CHAPTER

Saturday July 19, 1913

VERA MAE PEERS OUT OF HER BEDROOM WINDOW, WAITING for Reginald's motorcar to pull away from the house and disappear from sight. As soon as the coast is clear, she hitches up her skirt and hightails it to Reginald's private study, moving faster than any proper lady has ever moved before, all refinement gone to the wind.

"Do you have it?" she whispers, meeting Bennett at the locked door.

"Aye, milady." Bennett pulls the housekeeper's master key for the study out of her pocket. "The grumpy old bat's gonna go barmy when she finds out I've nabbed it." She unlocks the door. "Please let's be quick."

Vera Mae goes straight to Reginald's desk and tries the drawer containing the files he's gathered on Eulalie. It's locked.

"Damn it." She looks around for a tool to get inside, finds a silver paper knife with a narrow pointed tip, and prepares to jab it into the keyhole.

"Wait!" Bennett stops her. "Heavens, milady! If you have a prod of that in there, you'll do it some damage, then His Lordship will know someone's had a sneaky meddle."

"What do you suggest?" Vera Mae tosses the knife down.

"May I borrow some hairpins off you, milady?"

Vera Mae turns around, presenting her up-do for Bennett, happy to loosen a curl in the pursuit of the information she needs.

"That oughta do it." Bennett plucks out two pearl-tipped pins without disturbing a hair and proceeds to crouch in front of the drawer, twiddling the pins inside the lock.

"Wherever did you learn this trick?" Vera Mae watches, fascinated.

"You grow up in a family such as mine, you learn all sorts." Bennett pops the lock. "There you are, milady." She steps back.

"You are magic, Bennett." Vera Mae claps her hands together. "Thank you!"

She yanks open the drawer, fishes out the file, and pores over every page, seeing records of everything from the marriage of Olivia Chase to Percy Meux in 1908, up to a series of police and doctor's notes detailing the abuse Eulalie suffered at his hands, her various hospitalizations, and his subsequent convictions.

"What's milady looking for? If you don't mind my asking." Bennett stands by the door, listening out for any of the other staff. "I hope His Lordship isn't doing you no wrong."

"I'm the one doing wrong, Bennett. As you're well aware." Vera Mae flips through the whole file, searching for any mention of Flora, relieved when she finds none. "She's not here," she mutters to herself. "He doesn't know."

Already running late for a clandestine rendezvous with Eulalie, she scoops the file back together, replaces it in the drawer, and leaves the study in a hurry, instructing Bennett to telephone for a private cab at once.

"It's imperative that His Lordship does not find out about this." She consults her wristwatch, calculating how much time she has before Reginald returns. "He must not even know that I've left the house."

Twenty minutes later, the cab drops her off in front of a shop on Charing Cross Road in Westminster. A shop scarcely any man would dare to follow her into, should Reginald still have people on her tail.

It's called The Woman's Press, and it sells all manner of suffragette products in addition to the usual books and pamphlets. There's motoring scarves, bags, belts, tobacco pouches, white muslin summer blouses to wear on rallies and protests, and many other things besides. Even soap and chocolate. Nothing a man could want or need.

Outside, a volunteer wearing purple, white, and green wanders the street, selling copies of the WSPU's *Suffragette* newspaper from a satchel. She walks in the gutter rather than on the pavement to avoid being troubled by the police, though plenty passing men give her trouble enough, whispering foul things in her ear and pinching her bum. One young lad, on the urging of his friends, dashes up to her, punches her in the breast, then runs away. On the heels of that, an older gent declares himself to be a proud member of the National League for Opposing Woman Suffrage and thwacks her with his cane before walking on. All this she suffers without uttering a single cross word.

Vera Mae buys a copy of *The Suffragette* from her, wishes her well for the rest of the day, and ventures inside the shop. After perusing the shelves for a moment—so as not to appear suspicious, and to make sure nobody comes in behind her—she wanders to the cash register, smiling at the familiar face of the suffragette behind the counter.

"Hello, Connie." She glances once more outside, seeing nothing out of the ordinary. "Is Miss Sauvage here? Or has she left any message for me?"

Connie nods. "Come into the back."

She shows Vera Mae into a private parlor at the rear of the shop. There, Eulalie is awaiting her arrival with a posy of violets and a broad smile.

"You made it!" Eulalie presents her with the flowers. "Did you have any trouble getting away?"

"Not enough to stop me." Vera Mae melts into her arms, swiftly initiating a kiss of the most ardent nature.

"Oi, none of that here," Connie chastises the love-struck pair. "Clear off and get yourselves a room somewhere. Go on now!"

"I have one." Vera Mae beams up at Eulalie. "It's a modest little place Reginald doesn't know about, and I'm so excited to show you."

Eulalie has a hackney carriage waiting on a side street behind the shop, so they slink away unnoticed, Vera Mae providing the driver with an address in Mayfair. An address that turns out to be anything but little or modest.

"Bloody hell, Vera." Eulalie stands in the grand entrance hall of a palatial house in exclusively aristocratic Grosvenor Square, near Hyde Park. "Whose is this?"

"Up until quite recently, it was part of my family's estate. Nothing whatsoever to do with Reginald." Vera Mae sets her hat on the head of a decorative bronze statue by the staircase. "My family acquired it through marriage, but never had any use for it. It's always been kept tenanted, but the last tenants were given their notice earlier this month."

"Why?" Eulalie wanders into the drawing room and surveys a cabinet full of pointless ornaments.

"Because it is no longer deeded to my brother, the earl." Vera Mae flings her jacket and gloves onto the sofa. "It belongs to me."

"He gave it to you?" One hundred percent of Eulalie's attention is diverted to her. "This is what you've been planning?"

"I didn't want to tell you until it was all settled, which it now is." Vera Mae scoops up her hands and kisses her fingers, hoping for her approval. "With this property and the generous annuity willed to me by my late husband, we shall be quite comfortable."

"We?" Eulalie smirks.

"That's not too presumptuous of me, is it?" Vera Mae second guesses herself. "There's enough room for us all—you, me, Flora, and your mother—and the location is perfect. Hyde Park is just across the way—Flora would love it, I'm sure—and your studio is within walking distance. Furthermore, we can make sure your mother has the very best medical care here in London."

Eulalie doesn't appear to be entirely sold on the prospect. "Vera, the money ..."

"Oh, please." Vera Mae dismisses her concern. "If I told you the amount of my annuity, you would be ill with disgust." She places Eulalie's hands on her waist and wriggles into a hug. "Of course, we must first resolve this appalling business with your husband."

Eulalie's embrace weakens. "I don't know how." She pulls away and flops onto the sofa.

"I think I do." Vera Mae keeps a smile firmly pinned on her face. "Flora is safe for the time being—Reginald doesn't know about her, I'm certain of that—so I say we seek out your husband ourselves. Let's beat Reginald to the punch."

"And do what?" Eulalie upturns both palms.

"We'll pay him off." Vera Mae pulls a folded checkbook from her pocket, showing Eulalie the method by which she means to do so. "Whatever it takes. Let's make the bastard go away—preferably out of England—then Reginald will have nothing to hold over us."

Eulalie shakes her head. "If you give the man money once, he'll keep coming back for more. You'll never get rid of him. He'll bleed you dry."

"All right." Vera Mae clings to positivity, launching herself into her backup plan. "Then we'll sell this place and move to Paris. All four of us."

"Just like that?" Eulalie looks skeptical. "You want to run?" She scoffs at the idea. "I suppose you do realize there's a war brewing in Europe?"

"I'm trying, Lollie." Vera Mae's smile dissolves. "What more can I do? I've been racking my brain for a solution to this, and you're shooting me down on all fronts." She holds back tears, determined to remain strong. "I will not be parted from you. Do you hear me? I don't care who this man is, or how formidable an opponent he believes himself to be, I will *not* give you up."

Eulalie lets out a groan of frustration. "Well, France is not the answer. The threat of war aside, Paris was an adventure, but I do not wish to spend the rest of my life there."

"Canada, then." Vera Mae keeps trying. "We could—"

"No. Never." Eulalie flatly rejects the notion. "I will not allow you to put yourself on another transatlantic ship. Not after what you went through last year. It would be a torture."

Vera Mae's tears spill. "I would do *anything* for you."

"Not that." Eulalie shakes her head resolutely. "In any case, I don't want you to flee your home because of me. That isn't fair."

"Flee my home? Ha!" Vera Mae dries her eyes with a hanky. "Tigress, my family have disowned me, and the moment I leave Regent's Park, I will be cut off from society. What home do I have? There is nothing holding me here. Reginald will make sure to tell everyone what I've done. Forget Lady Darlington, I shall be known as the Baroness of Sapphistry: lesbian, suffragist, whore. And do you know what? I don't care. I don't give one good goddamn because I *love* you." She stomps her foot on the floor. "So stop being such a bloody pessimist and help me stand against this wretched man so that we can be together."

"God, you're beautiful when you're infuriated." Eulalie lunges for her waist, grabs her, and yanks her onto the sofa, eliciting a squeal of delight.

"Don't be naughty!" Vera Mae slaps her playfully.

"Naughty?" Eulalie holds her down on the overstuffed cushions. "You think this is naughty?" She targets Vera Mae's armpits with unrelenting tickles, setting off fits of uncontrollable laughter.

"Desist at once!" Vera Mae flails helplessly on her lap, both legs in the air, skirt crumpled up, stockings exposed. "This is so undignified!"

"I love you." Eulalie abates the tickles and kisses her. "I'm sorry for being such a miserable prick. You don't deserve that. You've done so much."

"You're worried for Flora." Vera Mae anchors her arm around Eulalie's neck and cuddles up to her. "I understand."

"That's no excuse." Eulalie cradles her. "I shouldn't make you bear the brunt of my frustration. Not ever." She pinches Vera Mae's soft lips between her own. "I want to live here with you. More than anything." Another kiss. "So we *will* find a way to make this happen, I promise. I just need more time to think. I'm not giving up."

"I shan't let you." Vera Mae rubs noses with her. "But I do wish everything weren't so bloody complicated. Life used to be so simple."

"Did it?" Eulalie cocks an eyebrow. "Perhaps for people like you. Not so much for those of us who've always lived in your shadow."

Vera Mae won't hear a word of that. "I don't think you live in anyone's shadow. I think you're the one casting the light for us all."

The compliment teases a smile from Eulalie's lips. "Even though things are far from easy, do you think we could manage one night? One perfect night." She pulls a pair of red, green, and white tickets from the chest pocket of her jacket. "There's a women's suffrage rally taking place in Hyde Park next weekend." She shows the tickets to Vera Mae. "Will you come? There'll be thousands upon thousands of people. We'll never be seen. And after ... I thought we might spend the night together. Would you be able to escape from Regent's Park for that long? I so desperately want to sleep with you. To go to bed with you in the evening, and wake up with you in the morning."

"It's not impossible." Vera Mae thinks carefully on it. "If I tell Reginald I'm going to spend a day or two at

Burley House, he wouldn't question it. In fact, he'd probably encourage me out the door." She tucks the tickets back into Eulalie's pocket for safekeeping. "We ought not to stay in London, though. Just in case."

"How about Kent?" Eulalie suggests tentatively. "I'm overdue a visit, and I think it's probably about time you met my daughter."

"Do you really mean it?" Vera Mae's eyes light up. "I would love to meet her! Your precious little girl."

"If you're certain Reginald will not find out," Eulalie cautions her. "Flora cannot be put at risk."

"I shall exercise the utmost vigilance," Vera Mae vows with absolute sincerity. "Now I have an offer of my own for you, Miss Sauvage." She toys with Eulalie's shirt buttons. "Would you like to see the master bedroom?"

Hours later, her body still flooded with endorphins after spending a significant portion of the day in bed with Eulalie, Vera Mae slinks back into the Regent's Park house mere moments before Reginald returns home, and promptly retires to her bedroom to change for dinner.

"Did everything go all right today, milady?" Bennett lays her mistress's evening dress out on the bed. "All was quiet while you were gone."

Vera Mae sits in front of her vanity, watching Bennett in the mirror, wondering how to broach a delicate subject. In truth, the afternoon did not go quite as she'd planned. Eulalie accepted a set of keys to the house readily enough, but until the looming threat of her husband can be permanently extinguished, their future together remains uncertain. Not only that, but if the worst should happen with Reginald, Eulalie would be in dire need of protection. Precautions must be taken to ensure her safety. Drastic measures must be considered.

"What did you mean earlier when you spoke about growing up in a family such as yours?" Vera Mae props her elbows on the vanity and clasps her hands in front of her face, smelling Eulalie's sex on her fingers. "What sort of family did you grow up in?"

Bennett shrugs. "You know how it is in the East End, milady."

"Not really." Having never set foot in the place, all Vera Mae knows of anything further east than Islington comes entirely from Dickens novels. "Tell me."

"Well, it's a harder life, to be sure." Bennett selects a pair of satin gloves to match the dress, not letting the conversation distract her from her work. "The line between right and wrong isn't always so clear."

"Is it anywhere?" Vera Mae twists to face her. "Do you have ... connections?"

Bennett falters. "Connections to what, milady? I'm not a bad 'un."

"Of course not, Bennett. Don't be so dramatic. You've been with me far too long for me ever to think anything like that." Vera Mae tries to word herself better. "I simply want to know if you are able to obtain things on the sly."

Bennett holds her hands up in surrender. "I'm no thief, milady. Never in my life."

"Oh, heavens, no." Vera Mae sighs. "I'm not explaining myself well at all." She raps her fingertips on the vanity, takes a deep breath, and forces the words out. "What I'm saying is: I need a gun, and I need you to get it for me. Will you do that?"

Bennett opens and closes her mouth several times before words come out. "I isn't all that sure as I proper understand you, milady." She chews on her lower lip. "You go shooting every year on the estate. You have a gun license yourself, so you may buy one any time you wish."

"Yes, I may, but then there would be a record of it, wouldn't there?" Vera Mae pauses to let that sink in. "If anyone were to inquire, I would be easily enough identified." She opens a drawer in the vanity and retrieves some crisp pound notes from a cloth purse. "So this gun—a revolver, with all the bits and bobs to go in it—must not be purchased, it must be … acquired." She sets the money on the vanity. "Do you follow me now, Bennett?"

"I believe so, milady." Bennett pockets the money. "When must it be done?"

"Within the week. Is that possible?" Vera Mae thinks of her impending visit with Flora and Eulalie's mother. "I don't plan on using it, but I must know that I am able to protect myself and others if the need arises."

Bennett nods. "Let's speak no more of it." She returns to the dress. "I thought you might like the lilac tonight. I know you has a partiality for the pink, but that's being laundered at the minute, and—"

"Thank you, Bennett." Vera Mae feels a great weight lifted from her chest to know that she'll have a means to defend Eulalie in the event of the worst. "Your loyalty means a very great deal to me. I know you do not agree with the choices I've made of late, yet you do anything I ask of you without complaint, and I am grateful."

"It isn't that I don't agree, milady." Bennett fusses with the dress. "I worry for you, that's all, and I feared this artist was leading you astray. But if that's not the case—if you was always inclined in such a way—I see no wrong in it. So long as she treats you right."

"Oh, she does." Vera Mae sucks the tip of her middle finger into her mouth, determined not to wash before dinner, loving the thought of sitting down at the table reeking of sex. "She's the one, Bennett. The only one."

CHAPTER

Saturday July 26, 1913

VERA MAE CHECKS HER APPEARANCE IN HER BEDROOM mirror, hoping she's suitably attired. As per Eulalie's instructions, she's chosen a simple white blouse and charcoal gray skirt for the Hyde Park suffragist rally. Nothing fancy. Nothing colorful. The aim of this basic dress code—options limited to smart outfits of white, gray, navy, or black—is to eliminate all bright colors except those of the NUWSS, which are to be painted on placards and worn on the women's sashes, hat badges, raffia cockades, and the haversacks from which leaflets are to be distributed to anyone who'll take one.

Behind her, Bennett places a small, cloth-wrapped bundle into a leather suitcase on the bed, tucking it in the folds of a silk nightgown. "Everything's packed for you, milady." She buckles the suitcase up and prepares to carry it downstairs. "Everything you requested." She hesitates. "Will there be anything else?"

Vera Mae doesn't get a moment to answer. The bedroom door swings open, thrust wide with such force that it hits the wall, tearing a hole in the silk wallpaper and putting a dent in the plasterwork beneath. Without so much as a knock or a beg-your-pardon, three footmen and Reginald's valet stride in, suitcases in hand, and begin packing up her things.

"What is the meaning of this?" she demands.

"They're acting on His Lordship's order, milady." The matronly housekeeper stands in the doorway, supervising the proceedings. "You, and anything belonging to you, is to be removed from the house directly."

"This is outrageous." Vera Mae snatches her coconut off one of the footmen. "I'm to tolerate these oafs rifling through my intimates?"

"It's His Lordship's order," the housekeeper repeats, refraining from making eye contact.

"Then His Lordship is a miserable, callous prick." Vera Mae hands the coconut over to Bennett. "Guard this for me." She shoves past the housekeeper, hitches up her skirts, and storms downstairs, barging into the breakfast room and disrupting Reginald's breakfast. "Explain yourself." She faces him with her arms crossed.

"Good morning, darling." He doesn't even look up from reading his new favorite book: *The Unexpurgated Case Against Woman Suffrage.* "Displeased, are we?"

Vera Mae wrenches the book from his hands and hurls it across the room. "Look at me, you heartless bastard. What have you done?"

"What've *you* done, Vera?" He meets her glare and gets up from the table, towering over her. "I just got off the telephone with Burley House. Given your recent peculiar behavior, I thought it best that I confirm the details of your visit." A smug smile spreads across his face. "Imagine my surprise when they informed me they had no record of your impending arrival."

"It's obviously a simple mistake." Vera Mae does her best to appear unconcerned, suppressing a pang of dread. "Why would you assume that I—"

"The mistake is yours, Vera." He cuts her off. "Spare me your lies."

"Very well." Vera Mae offers no apology, the dread hardening in her chest and turning to anger. "If only you would spare me your ignorance in return." She funnels her anger into defiance. "What is it that you want to know? That I am engaged to spend the night with Miss Sauvage? That my body yearns for her touch? That she makes me feel the way no man ever could? That she gives me such intense pleasures? Over and over and over again."

"Enough!" Reginald lashes out, swiping his full coffee cup off the breakfast table and into the nearest wall, the impact shattering it. "I warned you of the consequences of your actions, yet you have connived to commit sin with this invert. She has poisoned you with her sickness, now I have no choice but to inform her husband."

"Do it." Vera Mae spins on her heels and walks away from him. "I am done with this pointless charade. I shall return for my belongings tomorrow."

She collects her suitcase from the hall and heads straight for the Grosvenor Square house. There, she finds a plain white hat with a raffia cockade in NUWSS colors waiting for her on the writing desk in the parlor, next to a white sash displaying the union name in red and green. Elsewhere about, the portrait she commissioned Eulalie to paint is leaning against the wall, and several more paintings are scattered throughout the room, along with a bag of Eulalie's clothes and a pair of hastily kicked off boots.

"Hello?" she calls out. "Are you here, Tigress?"

The hurried padding of bare feet down the staircase heralds Eulalie's entrance, and she appears in the parlor wearing her painting clothes, her scruffy shirt untucked and lazily buttoned, her navel showing, her hair piled on top of her head, resembling a bird's nest. One look at her and Vera Mae can't feel anything but content and happy, despite her troubles at Regent's Park.

"You're making yourself at home." She greets Eulalie with a kiss. "I'm glad. I was worried when you took the keys that you were only doing so to be polite." She fishes a hanky out of her pocket and dabs at a fleck of blue paint on Eulalie's neck. "What are you painting? You're covered in the stuff."

"I couldn't sleep last night." Eulalie pulls her up the stairs and toward the bedrooms. "I kept thinking about Flora, and how moving to London is going to be such an upheaval for her. I want her to feel welcome the very minute she walks in—whenever that might be. I want her to feel like she belongs. Like there's a place here that was made just for her." She invites Vera Mae to step inside the nursery, where she's begun painting a mural on one wall. "I hope you don't mind. I suppose I should've asked."

The mural features a kaleidoscope of butterflies, a few cottontail rabbits, and an array of rainbow-colored hearts all surrounding Flora's name in large blue letters: Flora Mae.

"My goodness." Vera Mae cracks a smile. "We have the same middle name."

"We all do." Eulalie lolls against the doorjamb. "I was born Olivia Mae. So you know what that means, don't you? This really is fate." She tickles her fingers down Vera Mae's arm. "Do you like the mural?"

"It's perfect." Vera Mae's stomach flutters with excitement at the thought of them forming a family together. "I want Flora to be content here. She needs to have a space she knows is hers. A little sanctuary all her own." She turns to Eulalie, her excitement tinged with fear, not knowing what obstacles their future may yet be littered with. "I want this life with you so much." She seeks comfort in Eulalie's arms, not caring that she smells of turpentine. "We will make this work, won't we? Tell me we'll be together always."

"I want to spend the rest of my life with you, Vera. Do you doubt me?" Eulalie hooks Vera Mae's chin on her finger and tilts her head up. "I'll never want another woman." She initiates a deep, reassuring kiss, breaking it only when the need for air becomes vital. "I love you," she whispers. "Now let me wash up, then we'll head to the rally." She takes a few steps toward the bathroom, then hesitates. "You would tell me if anything was wrong, wouldn't you? You seem a little fraught. Did something happen at Regent's Park?"

Vera Mae shakes her head, determined not to spoil their weekend. "Everything's all right," she lies, managing to make herself sound suitably convincing. "I've been so looking forward to this night. Nothing will ruin it." Of that, she is certain.

As soon as Eulalie is clean and dressed, they don their NUWSS colors in the parlor—Vera Mae in the hat, Eulalie in the sash—and Vera Mae deposits her wedding ring in a decorative dish atop the fireplace mantel.

"It's a reminder of a life to which I no longer belong." She answers Eulalie's unspoken question. "Now let's not dawdle."

She takes Eulalie by the arm and they descend upon Hyde Park, soon realizing that they've vastly underestimated the size of the crowd.

"Oh, my God ..." Vera Mae clings tighter to Eulalie, struggling to summon enough courage to cross the street.

The Grand Entrance to Hyde Park—a massive stone gateway consisting of three carriage archways and two foot entrances, ornamented on all sides by fluted ionic columns—is swarming with people. It's a veritable suffrage army. Fifty thousand law-abiding suffragists of all ages have converged here from all over England, each and every one wearing her NUWSS colors proudly, some marching for the cause with their supportive husbands and children in tow.

A few have ridden bicycles to the rally, despite a prevailing myth perpetuated by men that the vibrations generated between a woman's legs in doing so could cause them to develop insatiable appetites for sexual pleasure, and may well result in lesbianism.

Outside the park, never missing an opportunity for recruitment, a WSPU Votes for Women bus is stationed by the gates, a horde of suffragettes leafleting people as they pass, and selling copies of their paper. One seller—advanced in years but bearing up bravely—has a copy snatched out of her hands by an anti-suffrage man and is beaten about the face with it several times before her comrades come to her rescue and shoo the beast away. As this happens, three more of their fellow suffragette warriors are chalking the pavement in the colors of the WSPU, writing out the demands of their cause before the police come to remove them.

Deeds, not words!

Equality for women!

Justice for women!

"Is it too much for you?" Eulalie responds to Vera Mae's clammy, trembling hands. "I'm sorry, this was thoughtless of me. We don't have to go on." She prepares to turn around. "There's going to be a special service at St. Paul's Cathedral tomorrow. Perhaps we could attend that instead?"

"No." Vera Mae prevents her from retreating. "I want to do this, and with you by my side, I know that I can." She plants Eulalie's arm firmly around her waist and clamps it there with her hand. "We shall proceed."

She takes a deep breath and steps off the curb, determined to face her fears, and together they navigate the ever-expanding ocean of human bodies in Hyde Park, slowly but surely making their way to speaker's corner, where they watch Millicent Fawcett—the eloquent president of the NUWSS—deliver a rousing speech from the back of a wagonette.

By the end of it, Vera Mae finds herself a full-fledged member of the NUWSS, as well as the Women's Freedom League, and before leaving the rally, she's also volunteered to sell copies of *The Vote* on the streets of Mayfair next week. She even keeps the NUWSS colors pinned on her hat when they go to catch their train at Paddington Station.

"I'm so proud of you." Eulalie steals a kiss from her as they enter an empty first class carriage—their tickets upgraded from third on Vera Mae's absolute insistence. "You're becoming a very strong woman. Stronger than me, I don't doubt. Before we met, I daresay you'd never have dreamed of wearing suffrage colors so boldly."

"Before we met, I was a caged woman." Vera Mae settles into the padded seats, one glimpse at the plain wooden benches in third being all she needed to convince herself that a little luxury, in this instance, was no less than a basic human right. "You released me." She slips a hand onto Eulalie's thigh, thrilled to find the dildo trapped there inside her trousers. "Is this for me?" She massages its length.

"Absolutely." Eulalie grins.

She leans in for another kiss, but draws back when the carriage door opens and a young man enters, seating himself opposite them.

"A little far from the stage, aren't we?" He laughs, mocking Eulalie's appearance.

Eulalie opens her mouth to respond, but Vera Mae has a quicker tongue.

"Is it a crime to dress as one pleases?" She keeps her hand on Eulalie's thigh. "No?" She raises a challenging eyebrow. "Then keep to your own. Our business is no concern of yours."

"No need to get your dander up, madam." The man holds his hands up in surrender, though still laughing. "I was just—"

"Being ignorant is what you were just and are." Vera Mae huffs indignantly. "If the sight of my friend displeases you, feel free to remove yourself to another carriage so that we may be spared the sight of you also."

That shuts him up, and rather than spend the next little while suffering her steely glare, he does indeed get up and remove himself.

"Arse," Vera Mae mutters under her breath. "Good riddance."

Overcome by such a fierce display of protectiveness, a tear comes to Eulalie's eye. "My heart swells with pride to be with you." She pecks Vera Mae's cheek. "You *are* a brave woman, no matter what you might think."

"We'll see." Vera Mae's mind turns to thoughts of Eulalie's husband. "I hope I can be brave enough when the moment comes."

CHAPTER

FROM A SMALL TRAIN STATION IN RURAL KENT, VERA MAE and Eulalie are met by the local bus service: a large, canopy-covered wagonette drawn by two stocky horses under the command of an aging farmer who also uses the wagonette for transporting hay when the need arises.

"This is quaint." Vera Mae wipes down one of the wooden benches with a hanky before sitting, sweeping off several stalks of hay and a wandering grasshopper.

"Welcome to humble country life." Eulalie slides onto the bench beside her, setting their suitcases at their feet. "Think you'll cope with our simple ways?"

"Don't poke fun at me." Vera Mae jabs her in the ribs. "I am quite capable of assimilating myself into your world, so don't you dare give me away to your mother. I do not wish for her to think me haughty. Your friends already think me haughty."

Eulalie chuckles. "My friends think everyone with a high collar and a proper pair of knickers to be rather la-di-da, so I wouldn't fret too much about that. But I shan't tell my mother who you really are. Not if you don't want me to. I shall refrain from introducing you as the Baroness of Sapphistry."

Another rib jab. "Hush." Vera Mae puts her hand on the bench between them, laying it over Eulalie's and weaving their fingers together for the rest of the bumpy, rambling journey to a thatched black-and-white cottage on a narrow dirt road surrounded by trees.

When the bus comes to a halt and lets them off, Eulalie debarks from the wagonette first, sets their suitcases on the ground, then helps Vera Mae down, lifting her from the bottom bar of the rickety steps and lowering her gracefully onto terra firma. In that same moment, Flora—keeping an eye on the road from her grandmother's kitchen window—bursts from the cottage door wearing her Sunday best and runs at full tilt down the paved garden path, her tiny arms outstretched.

"Mummy! Mummy!" She barrels into her mother.

"How's my sweet babe?" Eulalie picks her up and lavishes her with kisses. "I've missed you! Have you been a good girl for Grandma?"

Flora nods enthusiastically. "Me pretty dress. Look!" She shows off her favorite homemade summer frock, worn especially for her mother's visit. "You likes?"

"It's lovely, Florrie." Eulalie encourages her to make eye contact with Vera Mae. "Do you want to meet someone very precious to me?"

More nodding. "A princess?"

"Almost." Eulalie smirks. "But she doesn't want anyone to know, so it'll have to be our secret." She nuzzles Flora's nose. "Her name is Vera. Say hello."

Too shy to speak to the captivating stranger who's smiling so warmly at her, even if she is a sort of princess, Flora waves.

"Hello, my darling." Vera Mae beams. "Aren't you a beautiful little thing?" She fingers Flora's light blonde curls, fawning over her. "Just like your mother."

Flora giggles and blushes.

"Where's your grandma?" Eulalie sets her back on the ground, turns her in the direction of the cottage, and picks up the suitcases. "Go and fetch her."

"I do not need to be fetched," Eulalie's mother responds from the cottage doorway, leaning on the doorjamb, resting her hands on her cane. "I'm here, waiting patiently for my turn." She beckons them over.

Though not terribly old, she's frail. Too thin to be healthy, her well-worn clothes hang limply from her bony frame. A mop of straggly, graying hair is pinned up in a tight bun on top of her head, and she has a pair of wire-rimmed glasses perched on her nose. She looks like an austere governess, but there's no severity in her tone.

"You haven't come alone, I see." She peers at Vera Mae over her glasses. "You've brought a friend."

"Not a friend, Mother." Eulalie deposits the suitcases on the doorstep and brings Vera Mae forward, laying a gentle hand on her lower back. "This is Vera, my companion."

"Companion?" One of her mother's eyebrows shoots up. "Oh, at last!" She extends an unsteady hand to Vera Mae, offering a weak handshake. "Livvy hasn't ever brought anyone home to me or Flora. You must be very special indeed."

"I hope so." Vera Mae doesn't grip too hard for fear of breaking her. "It's a very great pleasure to meet you, Mrs. Chase."

"Nell, please. I've no use for formality." She ushers them inside, directing them all into the tiny, rustic cottage kitchen for glasses of fresh lemonade and exceedingly generous slices of cake.

Wanting to be close to her mother, Flora sits on Eulalie's lap rather than in her own chair and steals glances at Vera Mae between every mouthful of vanilla sponge, her shyness gradually giving way to curiosity.

"Cake good?" she asks, her face smeared with icing sugar.

"It's delicious." Vera Mae takes another forkful to prove it. "Did you help your grandma to bake this one?"

Flora bobs her head up and down, knowing better than to speak with her mouth full.

"Well, I think you're very clever indeed," Vera Mae praises her. "I've never made a cake before. Perhaps you can teach me one day. I'd like to make one for your mummy."

"Gamma!" Flora turns to her grandmother, eyes wide with excitement. "Make more cake? Pleeeeeeease."

"Dinner wants making first." Nell eats slowly, wielding her fork in her right hand and chewing carefully. "Ever made a meat pie?" she asks their guest.

The answer to that, of course, is a resounding no, and Vera Mae soon finds herself embroiled in the fine art of pie-making. Banned from helping, Eulalie watches with much amusement as Vera Mae bumbles her way through the process, learning the names of various kitchen utensils as she goes along.

"Anyone would think you'd never set foot in a kitchen before." Nell frowns at her, flabbergasted that she doesn't know the difference between a sieve and a colander.

"I'm sorry." Vera Mae looks forlornly at Eulalie. "I'm going to make a dreadful wife for you, aren't I? I'm not at all domesticated."

"Oh, you silly goose." Eulalie rises to console her. "My love for you is not dependent on how well you can make a pie." She thumbs a streak of flour from Vera Mae's cheek.

"Wife?" Nell breaks into a lopsided smile. "My goodness, it is serious between you." She whips Eulalie's backside with a dishcloth. "Shame on you for not bringing her to me sooner. Now take the pie out of the oven." She looks around for Flora. "Come here and wash your hands. No filthy monkeys allowed at the table. We must look our best. After all, it's not every day we have the aristocracy around for dinner." She winks at Vera Mae.

"Is it really so obvious?" Vera Mae slumps into a chair, her plan to integrate herself seamlessly into modest country life having failed miserably at the first hurdle.

"My dear woman, you have pearls in your hair and diamonds in your ears, and you're about as unfamiliar with the inside of a kitchen as I am with Buckingham Palace." Nell wields the colander as proof. "It's naught to be ashamed of. Many would give their right arm for a title and a hoist up into society. Though I am surprised your lot accept you forging a different path for yourself in matters of the heart."

"They don't." Vera Mae sighs, remembering what awaits her when they return to London. "I am no longer welcome in that world."

Nell looks from Vera Mae to Eulalie, then back to Vera Mae. "You chose love?"

"I did." Vera Mae smiles up at her tigress. "I chose your daughter over everything, and I don't in the least bit regret it." She rises from the table, whisks off the filthy cook's apron Nell put her in, and prepares to dish up dinner. "Now, who wants pie?"

Despite slightly over-boiled vegetables and a cake that comes out looking rather concave and oddly deformed, Vera Mae's first attempt at a family dinner goes down well. Post-dinner entertainment consists of card games in the parlor, the exchange of family stories, and a quick peek through the Chase family photograph album. To conclude the evening, Nell shows off the hunger strike medals given to her by the WSPU, along with a brooch designed by Emmeline Pankhurst herself and handed out to all brave suffragettes who have been imprisoned for the crusade.

"You make out like you've been on the frontlines of a war," Eulalie teases her.

"It *is* a war," Nell grumbles. "A war against the tyranny of men!" She wags a finger at her daughter. "You should understand that better than anyone."

Eulalie's jaw tenses. "Don't start on that with me now, Mama. Not this weekend. This weekend is about me, Vera, and Flora—*not* him."

Responding to the anger in her voice, Flora gazes up from Eulalie's lap and yawns, rubbing her eyes. "You cross, Mummy?"

"No, my love." Eulalie softens her tone. "I think it's your bedtime, though." She gets ready to carry Flora up to bed, but Vera Mae keeps her on the sofa.

"Wait." She dashes to her suitcase in the hall. "I have something for Flora."

From its safe place tucked between two dresses, she pulls a girl's doll. Its porcelain head is topped with ringlets of honey-colored hair, its stuffed cloth body covered with a knitted dress.

"Oh, Vera ..." Eulalie watches Flora's eyes light up. "You're spoiling her already."

"This doll was mine when I was your age." Vera Mae presents the immaculately kept toy to Flora. "I knitted her a new dress just for you."

"Oooo!" Flora clasps the doll to her chest, then throws herself at Vera Mae, flinging her clumsy arms around Vera Mae's neck. "Thanks you!"

"You're very welcome." Vera Mae wraps Flora up in a hug, holding a living child in her arms for the first time. "Oh, my darling, you're so precious." She buries her face in Flora's hair, her need for the love of a child so palpable it brings a tear to Nell's eye.

"You have no children of your own?" Nell backhands the tear away.

"My child died last year." Vera Mae reins in her emotions and turns to Eulalie. "May I help you put Flora down for the night?"

"I'm sure she would like that very much." Eulalie helps Vera Mae off the sofa with Flora, retrieves their suitcases, and leads the way up the narrow, twisted staircase to the tiny bedrooms above.

After the mandatory brushing of teeth and a quick bedtime story by candlelight, Flora nods off with the doll in her arms, tucked up safe and sound under a quilt made by Nell.

"I am quite besotted with her," Vera Mae whispers, watching her sleep.

"I'm glad." Eulalie draws her out onto the landing. "I know she cannot ever replace what you have lost, but I promise you this: no child could ever love you more than she surely will."

She closes the bedroom door softly and plants a kiss on Vera Mae's lips, their moment of intimacy cut short when Nell hobbles up the stairs on her way to bed and catches them in the act, causing Vera Mae to withdraw like a misbehaving child fearing rebuke.

"Don't be shy." Nell chortles. "You aren't the first comely thing I've caught her necking. She's been wooing pretty skirts since she was old enough to know what it was all about."

"Mama ..." Eulalie rolls her eyes.

"What? Isn't it the truth?" Nell shuffles past with her cane. "First it was that nice young flower girl, then you came home with a barmaid. You know what our postman used to call you? Olivia Mae Chase Girls."

"Goodnight, Mother." Eulalie pulls Vera Mae into the guest bedroom: a cramped space filled with a double bed, an armoire, a washstand, a vanity, and a side table on which an oil lamp sits, providing the room's only source of light.

"Which one of us is to sleep here?" Vera Mae sees both of their suitcases on the floor.

"We both are." Eulalie casts off her waistcoat, ducking to avoid smacking her head on the slanted ceiling as she fills the washbasin with steaming hot water recently brought up from the kitchen in a large ewer.

"Together?" Vera Mae keeps her voice low, as if someone disapproving might be listening. "Your mother truly won't mind?"

"Not even a smidgen," Eulalie assures her. "In fact, she's the most liberal woman you're ever likely to meet. Of a love such as ours, she once told me: 'Feel no shame. We've all had a go. Some take to it more than others.'"

Vera Mae stifles a laugh, covering her face with her hands. "I really don't want to think about your mother 'having a go' with anyone."

"Nor do I." Eulalie delves a hand inside her trousers to adjust herself. "But the point is: we're as good as married in my mother's eyes, and what married couple wouldn't share a bed for the night?" She faces Vera Mae, the dildo now propped up to create a husband's bulge. "A wife must tend to her duties after all."

Vera Mae blushes. "Your cock does look mightily in need of release."

"Oh, how I've longed to hear such crudeness from your genteel lips." Eulalie beams. "Say more."

"How much more?" Vera Mae's cheeks turn a deeper shade of red as she fondles the bulge. "Arse and buggery." She unfastens Eulalie's trousers and pulls the dildo out. "Prick." She fists it again. "Cunt." She lets the tip poke at her mound. "*My* cunt." She dips her hand in the basin, scoops out some water, and douses the phallus with it. "Fuck." She gets the instrument hot and wet. "Fuck me." She pauses. "Now."

In the grip of lust, Eulalie tears off Vera Mae's clothes, wrenching open her blouse and the camisole beneath it, sending buttons scattering everywhere, many lost forever between the gaps in the old floorboards. Her skirt gets trampled beneath their feet. Her petticoat suffers a rip in Eulalie's haste to cast it off. Her knickers end up dangling from the corner of the armoire.

"I want you inside me," Vera Mae mewls, tumbling onto the bed in her chemise and corset, her knees drawn up and spread wide, ready to receive Eulalie's dripping priapus. "Do it to me."

Ornamented only with the imitation appendage, Eulalie moves into position above her and eases the tapered head into her lubricious sex.

"God, it's big." Vera Mae groans, her body stretching to accommodate the intrusion.

Once the crown pops through, the shaft glides easily into her tight channel, filling her inch by inch, the hot glass piercing her as if it were flesh.

"Oh, my Lord ..." Vera Mae gapes at the operation, watching the full length of the thing disappear inside her body. "We are united!"

"Do you like it?" Eulalie tests one gentle thrust, withdrawing only a few inches before hilting herself again.

"Give me more," Vera Mae pleads, cupping and kneading Eulalie's breasts, encouraging her to move harder and faster. "More!"

She matches the rhythm of Eulalie's exertions, raising her hips to meet every plunge, her cries of pleasure muffled by kisses, her paroxysm building deep within her core and cresting with such intensity that she forgets to breathe, her entire body quivering around Eulalie, vows of love whispered on her lips.

CHAPTER

Sunday July 27, 1913

FOR THE FIRST TIME IN HER ADULT LIFE, VERA MAE WAKES up relaxed, knowing there's no hurry to rise, no obligation to take breakfast at a certain time, and no need to dress especially for the occasion. And it's a fine day. The room is drenched in sunlight, the small eastward-facing window catching all the sun's early rays. Better yet, Eulalie is lying next to her.

Already awake and half dressed in yesterday's shirt, Eulalie snuggles closer and sneaks a hand up her chemise, fondling one of her charms. "Good morning, my beauty." She teases the nipple stiff. "There's fresh water in the ewer, and my mother's downstairs making breakfast."

Vera Mae murmurs happily. "This feels good." She dips one hand beneath the counterpane and explores Eulalie's naked sex. "I like waking up with you."

"The feeling is mutual." Eulalie parts her legs, inviting Vera Mae deeper.

"I could lie here in this bed with you forever." Vera Mae pushes two fingers inside her. "And I just might have to, because I fear I may have lost the ability to walk. You've been far too vigorous with me throughout the night."

"Entirely at your behest." Eulalie relinquishes Vera Mae's breast and reciprocates her southern attentions. "Do you not recall that you begged me for it each and every time?" She mirrors Vera Mae's probing tickles. "I'm exhausted because of you."

"You have such stamina." Vera Mae lets the palm of her hand repeatedly bump Eulalie's engorged clit. "You're a stallion with that wicked thing strapped to you."

"I'm paying for it this morning." Eulalie targets a special place within her, stirring up another orgasm from the depths of her sex. "My arse is killing me."

Vera Mae strives to touch Eulalie in the same way, her slender fingers finding that spongy button of flesh for the first time and exciting it relentlessly. Though her wrist tires and aches, she persists until they're both a bundle of trembling limbs, moaning against each other's mouths, their hushed climaxes arriving in unison.

In the wake of it, Vera Mae rolls Eulalie onto her back and settles against her chest, using one of her breasts as a pillow. "I do believe I've been fully initiated into this lesbian business."

"You've shown a great deal of enthusiasm for the work," Eulalie concurs, giving Vera Mae a congratulatory pat on the derrière. "Why did you never seek the love of a woman before? A dalliance with a maid at very least."

"I feared my father and would not shame my husband." Vera Mae sighs. "It isn't possible for something so scandalous to remain a secret in that world, and he was a good man. It was no fault of his own that I couldn't love him the way a wife ought. In any case, I'm happy to have saved myself for you." She squeezes Eulalie tighter, but recoils into her own space when the door creaks open and nightgown-clad Flora skips in, leaping straight onto the bed to cuddle her mother, her new doll clutched in her hand.

"Good morning, Florrie." Eulalie sits up and pulls Flora onto her covered lap. "Did you sleep well? And have lots of nice dreams?"

Flora nods, but her brow furrows with concern. "Better now?" she asks Vera Mae. "You had the scares."

"The what, love?" Vera Mae looks to Eulalie for a translation.

"You heard Vera making noises in the night?" Eulalie guesses, holding back a smirk.

Flora nods again. "Bad scares."

"Oh, dearie me." Vera Mae keeps the bed covers pulled up to her chin. She wants to sink under the counterpane and hide, but Eulalie tackles Flora's innocent curiosity without awkwardness or hesitation.

"Listen, darling. Sometimes, when grownups love each other very much, they sleep together—like Vera and Mummy. It doesn't mean Vera has the scares, so if you ever hear those sounds again, you needn't be worried." She kisses Flora's wrinkled forehead. "Just know that Mummy's taking ever such good care of Vera. All right, my sweet?"

Flora accepts that easily.

"Now, I'm afraid we must go back to London today." Eulalie doesn't leave pause for sadness to creep in. "But I have an idea. How would you feel about coming to live with me and Vera someday soon? There's a bedroom waiting for you. Would you like that?"

Flora perks up, nodding vigorously. "And Gamma?"

"Of course Grandma, too! Why don't you hurry to the kitchen and tell her?" Eulalie helps Flora off the bed. "Vera and I will be down for breakfast shortly."

"Gamma! Gamma!" Flora runs for her grandmother, her tiny feet thudding down the staircase. "Lunnon! We go Lunnon!"

"Are you sure that was wise?" Vera Mae frets in the quiet that follows. "We don't yet know when she'll be able to join us safely."

Eulalie shrugs, rising and pulling on her knickers and trousers. "It doesn't matter. She has very little concept of time."

"But your mother does." Vera Mae forces herself out of the warm, cozy bed, plucks her knickers off the corner of the armoire, and looks around the floor for the rest of her under things. "Where's my corset? Have you seen it?" She checks under the bed. "Wherever did it end up after you wrested it from my heaving bosom last night?"

"I thought you might wear this today instead." Eulalie pulls a lingerie box from her suitcase and sets it upon the vanity. "Don't let it give you too much of a fright."

Expecting something naughty like the French knickers, Vera Mae opens the box with caution, bemused to find that it contains a garment of the most unusual form. "Whatever is this devilish contrivance?" She holds it up, revealing it to be two bust gores anchored to elasticated shoulder straps and supported by a wide under-bust band that clasps at the rear center.

"Oh, if I could only take a picture of your face." Eulalie chuckles, amused by her clear distaste for the thing. "It's a brassiere. Have you never seen one before?"

"It is French, yes?"

"*Oui.*" Eulalie grins.

"Those bloody French again." Vera Mae lays it back in the box, still pondering it. "It isn't the most attractive thing I've ever seen."

"I'm not asking you to banish your corsets completely." Eulalie lifts off her chemise and helps her put the brassiere on. "I'm merely suggesting that you reserve them for bedtime." She drops a kiss on Vera Mae's neck. "They're sexful but wholly impractical. Especially when running around after a toddler."

Vera Mae inspects her reflection in the small wall mirror. "It does keep them up rather well." She takes a deep breath, expanding her lungs to full capacity. "And I suppose it will be nice to breathe properly for more than a few hours each day."

"I want you to be comfortable." Eulalie hands her a lacy camisole from the box so that she might cover the brassiere up. "And no-one will ever know you're wearing it."

Keeping an open mind, Vera Mae completes her dressing routine and takes another look in the mirror, wondering what to do with her tousled auburn braid. Bennett always sees to her more intricate up-dos. The most she can manage on her own is a simple bun, and she doubts Eulalie can be of any help. She watches with amazement as Eulalie scoops her windswept mane up with a ribbon, securing the dense mop on her head in a scruffy heap without ever reaching for so much as a hairpin.

"Do your tresses ever see a brush?" Vera Mae wonders, gasping when Eulalie seizes her by the waist and embraces her.

"Not often." Eulalie nibbles on her earlobe. "I'm hungry. Are you hungry?"

Vera Mae isn't listening. She's too preoccupied with the sensation of Eulalie's hands around her middle.

"I can feel the warmth of your hands on me, even through all these layers."

"And I can feel *you*." Eulalie caresses her shapely body. "I can hold you properly." She pulls Vera Mae close. "I can fondle you at will." She cups her hands around Vera Mae's newly accessible breasts. "You don't need to wear armor around me."

"Stop that." Vera Mae slaps her hands away. "You'll make me lewd." She consults her reflection in the mirror once more, making sure her nipples aren't showing. "Now, where is the water closet? I have a need that cannot be adequately met by that repugnant Victorian device of discomfiture." She points at the chamber pot tucked beneath the bed.

Pinching her lower lip between her teeth to prevent a laugh from escaping, Eulalie indicates for Vera Mae to look out the window. There, at the bottom of the back garden, is a tiny wooden shed: an old privy.

"Oh, my God. Are you joking?" Vera Mae stares aghast. "This is pure torture."

She leaves with a sigh of resignation, takes care of her necessaries in record time, and returns to the bedroom at double speed, promptly declaring:

"Never again!" Her cheeks flare cherry red. "I sat on a slug!"

Once the hilarity of that dies down—Eulalie being sworn to absolute secrecy on the matter—they finish preening and arrive for breakfast as Flora's demolishing a slice of jam-slathered toast, her fingers and face covered in more jam than likely made it into her mouth.

"Thank goodness you're here." Nell welcomes them to the table. "Florrie's got it into her head that she's going to live with you in London, bless her. She won't take no for an answer from me, so you'll have to put her right before she starts packing her bags."

"But it's true," Eulalie confirms the offer and helps herself to some toast. "We want both of you to come and live with us ... eventually."

"Where?" Nell's tone hardens.

"I have a house in London." Vera Mae fills the silence when Eulalie doesn't respond. "My brother gave it to me as a parting gift."

Less than thrilled by this news, Nell gives Flora a light prod with her cane and sends the child off to wash her hands and face, then fixes a scowl on her daughter.

"Do not get that girl's hopes up." She smacks a slice of toast out of Eulalie's hand. "You know she isn't safe with you."

"That won't always be true." Eulalie loses her toast to the cat.

"No?" Nell challenges her. "Then what are you going to do to fix it?"

Eulalie remains silent.

"That's what I thought." Nell eases herself into a chair, her anger giving way to despair. "This is all your wretched father's fault. He hadn't the brains God gave to a gnat. I'm glad he's gone to the grave, and I don't mind saying it." She turns to Vera Mae. "Excuse my frankness, but he became a right nasty little shite after our Eddie went."

"Who's Eddie?" Vera Mae seeks the answer from Eulalie.

"My brother." Eulalie attempts a second piece of toast. "He died."

"Eddie was my husband's perfect child and Livvy was mine." Nell smiles warmly at her daughter. "I knew the way she was, even as a littlin. She'd come home from school, tear off her dress, and change straight into her brother's britches. Then we lost the boy to that blasted war in South Africa, and the old man lost his sense. He started giving her such beatings for wearing those britches, and set his mind to fixing what he saw as being wrong in her head. Found her a man who'd treat her the same way he did. Knock it out of her, he said. Bloody fool."

"Must we talk about this now?" Eulalie abandons her toast.

"We must talk about it sometime." Nell won't let the topic rest. "Your father's left you with this curse: this man who won't be got rid." She huffs. "He wants shooting if you ask me, and I'd do it myself only I haven't the strength in my hands."

"I will fight for her," Vera Mae proclaims vehemently. "I am not afraid of this man."

"You might not be, but she is." Nell tips her head to Eulalie. "She'll never stand to him."

"Perhaps she doesn't have to." Vera Mae holds Eulalie's hand on the tabletop. "There is another way. It's not exactly what one would call legal, which is why I haven't hastened to consider it, but it may be decidedly more effective than the courts."

"What is it?" Eulalie's interest is piqued.

"Well, to be blunt, I am not a woman to be trifled with. I am a baroness and the daughter of an earl, and my brother is likely to be the next Viceroy of India. All of that is good for precisely one thing: influence over others."

"And?" Eulalie urges her to explicate.

"In short, it's not entirely outside the realm of possibility that, with a few well-placed words and some generous financial donations, I could orchestrate his permanent removal from the country." Vera Mae injects a healthy dose of confidence into her voice. "I might even have him transported to Australia, which would be no less than what he deserves."

"Do you really think you could?" Eulalie sounds painfully hopeful.

"It happens all the time. Why not for us? I know all the right people." Vera Mae weaves her fingers through Eulalie's, locking their hands together. "I'm going to do whatever it takes to keep you and Flora safe," she promises. "Which sounds quite valiant on the face of it, but is really rather selfish because I simply want to have you both all to myself."

"Call it whatever you like." Eulalie leans forward and kisses her. "Flora and I are lucky to have you in our lives."

CHAPTER

THE EVENING JOURNEY BACK TO LONDON IS SPENT LARGELY in quiet contemplation. Vera Mae ponders how in the world to follow through on her promise to Eulalie before Reginald tarnishes her reputation, while Eulalie focuses her creative mind on sketching plans for the rest of the mural on Flora's new bedroom wall. It isn't until they step into a hackney carriage and Vera Mae requests they be taken to the Regent's Park house that Eulalie questions her sudden willingness to consider more desperate measures.

"What are we doing here, Vera?" she asks as they pull up outside. "Are you not afraid that you'll be seen with me?"

"Wait here. I shan't be long." Vera Mae pecks her cheek and steps out of the motorcar. "I have a few things to pick up, that's all. Then we'll go back to Grosvenor Square."

Prepared for hostilities, she rings the bell and strides past the butler as soon as he opens the front door. No greeting. No pleasantries. Her belongings—suitcases, hatboxes, and miscellany—are heaped together in the entrance hall, and Bennett is slumped forlornly on her own little steamer trunk beside the pile, dutifully clutching the coconut to her chest.

"What is the meaning of this?" Vera Mae approaches the bedraggled maid, horrified to see her in such a state. "Have you been sitting there this entire time?"

"Yes, milady." Bennett rises, smothers a yawn, and makes a hopeless attempt to flatten the creases out of her apron. "His Lordship said for me to keep to this very spot until you returned."

"All night and all day?" Vera Mae can't quite believe it.

Bennett nods. "I've not had a wink of sleep."

"Did I not make myself clear?" Reginald appears from the library. "I want everything of yours removed from this house. Including that." He points at Bennett. "I have no use for her, and I assume she's been complicit in your machinations."

"Is there no limit to your cruelty?" Vera Mae glowers at him. "It is me you wish to punish, yet you find pleasure in the pain and degradation of those around me."

She turns her back on him and summarily instructs the footmen to load her possessions into and onto the waiting motorcar—as much as will fit.

"What about me, milady?" Bennett looks down at the battered trunk containing all of her meager personal effects, the worn leather now bearing the imprint of her bum. "Where am I to go?"

"Not to worry, Bennett." Vera Mae relieves her of the coconut. "If you wish to remain in my employ, you will not be cast aside."

Bennett perks up. "Thank you ever so, milady." She curtseys. "I would dearly love to remain in service to you."

"Then it is done." Vera Mae beams. "Be patient just a short while longer, yes? I shall send the motor back pronto to rescue you from this godforsaken pit of doom, along with the rest of my things and the last dregs of my swiftly diminishing sanity."

She turns to leave, but Reginald halts her.

"There is one other thing, my dearest." He pulls two pearl-tipped hairpins from his jacket pocket. "Are you able to guess where I found these?"

Vera Mae's heart drops into the pit of her stomach.

"I wondered what it could be that you were looking for, so I went through the file again and found something curious in your invert's medical records." Reginald twirls the hairpins between his fingers. "There's a child, isn't there?"

Vera Mae grits her teeth and snatches the hairpins from him. "Go to hell!"

Her business at the house concluded, she doesn't tarry. As the footmen finish affixing one last trunk onto the motorcar, she puts on a smile and clambers into the backseat, coconut in hand, distressed to see that Eulalie's mood has turned uncharacteristically grim.

"What's wrong, my love?"

"You tell me." Eulalie clenches and unclenches her jaw, her body rigid with tension, like a rabbit preparing to bolt from a fox. "Reginald knows you've been seeing me again, doesn't he? He's given you your marching orders. That's what this little detour is about."

"I didn't let on." Vera Mae pleads no fault, opting to keep Reginald's latest revelation to herself for the time being. "He found out on his own when he called Burley House to confirm that they were expecting me." She rubs Eulalie's arm, hoping to soften her. "Please don't be angry. There was nothing I could've done."

"You knew of this before we left for Kent?" Eulalie flinches from her touch, backing into the corner of the seat and out of her reach. "When were you going to mention it?"

"I didn't want to ruin our night together." Vera Mae scoots closer, refusing to accept her retreat. "Please, darling." She snatches up one of Eulalie's hands. "This changes nothing."

"This changes *everything*." Eulalie wrenches her hand free. "I cannot stay in London."

Vera Mae shakes her head. "He doesn't know about the Grosvenor Square house." She grips Eulalie's jacket, determined to keep hold of her. "You're safe there."

"That's easy for you to say." Eulalie pries her away. "Percy isn't coming for *you*."

Rejected, Vera Mae clutches the coconut for comfort. "I won't let him hurt you."

"What are you going to do to stop him?" Eulalie bites back tears. "Once he gets to London, it'll only be a matter of time before he finds me, and you're no match for his fists."

A heavy silence descends upon them, and as soon as they get back to the Grosvenor Square house, Eulalie makes herself scarce. She draws a hot bath while Vera Mae oversees the delivery of her luggage into the entrance hall—first one load, then the second, an awe-struck Bennett arriving with the latter.

"This place is splendidly grand, milady." She walks lightly on the marble floor, as if afraid to crack it. "Where shall I bed down for the night?"

"I'll show you." Vera Mae leads her to the small, sparse servants' bedrooms in the attic. "You look ready to drop, so get some rest. We'll discuss your new duties here in the morning."

She bids Bennett goodnight and goes in search of Eulalie, finding her in Flora's bedroom, perched on the bed in camisole and knickers, gazing at the half-finished mural.

"It's getting late." She hovers in the doorway. "Are you coming to bed?"

No answer.

Before retiring alone and miserable, she makes one more attempt to engage her disconsolate companion. "I love you, Lollie. With all my heart."

"I know you do." Eulalie doesn't take her eyes off the mural. "But that's not enough."

Glad that she spoke, even if she can't bring herself to reciprocate the sentiment, Vera Mae pounces on her willingness to open the lines of communication once more.

"There *is* a way to fix this." She drops to her knees at Eulalie's feet, begging for her forgiveness. "Let's not forget, I know a married viscount who sleeps with prostitutes in cheap houses of assignation." She lays her head in Eulalie's lap. "I'm quite sure he'd be happy to do me a small favor in exchange for keeping that on the hush."

"You're going to blackmail a viscount into having my husband transported?" Eulalie raises both eyebrows. "That's your big plan?" She brushes Vera Mae off her like one would shove away an unwanted cat. "Do you have any idea how utterly ludicrous that sounds?"

Vera Mae stays on her knees, slumped over the bed. "Maybe it is, but I don't want to lose you." She longs for reassurance, but receives none.

After an excruciating silence, she gets up, wipes away her tears, and goes to bed, expecting nothing. Weary and dejected, she slips into her best silk nightgown, lets down her hair, and locks herself away in the master bathroom to conduct her nightly ablutions, relieved to have the miracles of modern plumbing available to her again, including a flushing toilet and hot water straight from the tap. When she returns to the bedroom, resigned to sleeping alone, her heart thrums to see Eulalie tucked up under the covers.

"Darling ..."

A spark of hope ignites in her again, and she stands at the side of the bed, knowing that the warm light cast upon her by the bedside lamp renders her nightgown obscenely translucent, the dark shadow of her pubic hair visible behind the pale silk.

"Will you look at me?" she asks, gripping the nightgown's lacy hem in her hand and bunching it at her hip, causing shimmering folds to cascade downward.

Eulalie's eyelids flutter.

She waits.

Once Eulalie's attention is fixed on her, she pulls off the nightgown and drops it to the floor, standing there stark naked, presenting herself for ocular evaluation.

"Do you want me tonight?" She runs her hands over her soft, curvaceous body. "I am every bit yours for the taking. Let me make you happy."

Eulalie says nothing, but flings the counterpane down, inviting intimacy.

Accepting that invitation, even though it lacks her usual fervor, Vera Mae crawls onto the bed, rolls Eulalie over, and tugs off her French knickers before spreading her legs to bare her manicured mound and the delicious treasure below. Then Eulalie changes her mind.

"Wait, stop," she protests unconvincingly. "I'm not sure I'll be able to ..." Her words dissolve into a wail as Vera Mae dips between her thighs.

"Mmm," Vera Mae moans into her succulent flesh. "I love your sex." She sucks Eulalie's fattened clit into her mouth, swirling her eager tongue around the hardened protuberance before releasing it with a kiss. "You taste divine."

She parts Eulalie's slick labia with her thumbs and drives her tongue deep into the pink, her unbridled ministrations bringing Eulalie to the pinnacle of her pleasure in minutes. But that doesn't sate her. She wants more, and as soon as Eulalie's paroxysm has waned, she straddles her lover and demands attentions of her own.

Words aren't necessary. She places one of Eulalie's hands on her left breast and directs the other to her core, guiding two fingers inside her gushing channel. Once impaled, she rocks herself to pleasure on those embedded digits, weeping from beginning to end.

Vera Mae wakes in the middle of the night, momentarily forgetting where she is. Nothing looks familiar. Especially not when it's bathed in moonlight.

Intending to help herself to a reassuring cuddle, she wriggles around and extends her arms, fumbling for a warm body that isn't there. She's alone. The sheets are cold.

Concerned that Eulalie's moping in Flora's bedroom again, she heaves herself out of the four-poster with a yawn and pads barefoot down the hall, guessing she'll find Eulalie curled up on Flora's bed. But the nursery's empty.

Perplexed, she wanders through the whole house, checking the kitchen in case Eulalie got up for something to drink, the parlor in case she couldn't sleep and went in search of a book to read, and the drawing room in case she sought to raid the liquor cabinet.

Eulalie is nowhere to be found.

Her unease escalating, Vera Mae traipses back to the bedroom, turns on the light, and searches in earnest for Eulalie's suitcase. It's missing. Her clothes are gone, and her toothbrush has been taken from the bathroom. There's no trace of her.

"No ... please, no ..."

Fearing that she's gone back to the studio to lie in wait for her husband, Vera Mae hurries into yesterday's clothes—brassiere and all. Since everything else is packed away downstairs, she delves through the suitcase she took to Kent and pulls out a jacket. As she does so, a heavy, cloth-bound object tumbles free and clatters to the floor.

It's the gun.

She unwraps it, checks that it's loaded, and slips it into her jacket pocket. Not caring to bother with hat and gloves, she leaves the house and dashes to the studio, her unrestrained hair billowing behind her, her skirt hitched up above her ankles, her heels clacking on the pavement, the sound echoing in the empty streets.

At Eulalie's building, she barges through the street door and runs up the stairs, never once stopping for breath.

The studio door is ajar.

"Lollie?" she calls out, pushing it open.

The studio is in darkness. There's no sign of Eulalie.

Afraid that she's too late, and not knowing what to do next, she collapses on the sofa, sobbing into her hands. Then she hears the striking of a match and the inhalation of breath. Cigarette smoke permeates the air, and there are footsteps. Heavy footsteps.

"Left you, has she?" A man's deep, gravelly voice comes from the darkened bedroom area beyond the heavy curtain. "I know what that's like."

The curtain moves back and Percy Meux emerges. Tall and heavyset, he's a hairy beast of a man whose weight easily doubles Vera Mae's, and she has no doubt that he's capable of killing someone with a single punch. His large hands are scarred from so many past fights, the skin of his knuckles fresh and pink, still healing from his latest brawl.

"You're the swank bitch my woman's been dipping her finger's in, aintcha?" He flicks cigarette ash on the floor. "She's always had good taste in cunt, I'll give her that."

"She is *not* your woman." Vera Mae rises from the sofa and backs away. "Not anymore."

"Is that right?"

When he steps into the beam of a streetlight spilling in through the windows, Vera Mae gets a better look at his chubby face. The lower half is covered with a thick beard and mustache, the bridge of his nose is bent and misshapen, and he has sinister, beady eyes.

Disliking the lecherous way he looks at her, she retreats steadily, but stumbles in the darkness. The heel of one shoe catches on the corner of a blanket dangling from the arm of the sofa and trips her up, sending her flailing to the floor, landing with a squeal atop the pile of cushions still heaped there, her skirt rucked up around her knees.

He looms over her.

Panicked, she drives a hand into her pocket, fishing for the gun, but it slips from her grasp and she loses it between the cushions. She's defenseless.

"Do you know why I'm here?" He crouches beside her.

"You want Olivia." Vera Mae gropes blindly for the gun, trying to do so with her arm twisted awkwardly behind her back, obscuring the movement. "But she is not yours to take."

"You've got me all wrong, love." Percy slaps a hand over his heart, feigning hurt. "You're welcome to my leavings." He sucks on his cigarette, ash dropping on Vera Mae's blouse. "I ain't here for that worthless little fucktress."

"What then?" Vera Mae winces, her arm strained at an unnatural angle. "What's brought you out from under your rock?"

She doesn't see it coming. In a flash, Percy's hand is on her neck, his fat fingers wrapped around her throat, compressing her carotid arteries.

"Where's my child?" he snarls. "It ain't right that the littlin's being kept from me."

Vera Mae struggles in his vise-like hold. Her search for the gun abandoned, she chokes for air, kicking and thrashing beneath him, beating at his thick arm, trying to pry away his fingers. She's not strong enough. Her vision blurs. She sees a figure standing in the open doorway, silhouetted against the hallway light. Then a voice. A female voice.

"Leave her alone!"

Percy's attention is diverted. The pressure on Vera Mae's neck releases. She coughs and sputters, gasping for oxygen as Percy rises up, crushes the butt of his cigarette beneath his shoe, and steps toward the statuesque stranger.

Not a stranger. Vera Mae's eyes regain focus, equilibrium returning. It's Eulalie! She's standing on the threshold of the room, her suitcase at her feet, and Percy is advancing on her.

Renewing her search for the gun with a heightened sense of desperation, Vera Mae's grappling fingers finally find the grip. She wraps her hand around it, yanks it from the cushions, and cocks the hammer.

There's a click.

Percy turns his head.

She squeezes the trigger.

EPILOGUE

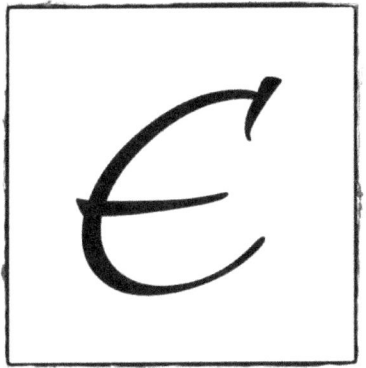

Monday August 3, 1914

S ITTING CONTENTEDLY ON A BLANKET UNDER THE SHADE OF a tree in Hyde Park, the remnants of a picnic lunch packed away in a wicker basket beside her, Vera Mae watches Flora skip about on the grass, trying to catch a small blue butterfly in her hands. Nearby, two little boys play war games with toy planes, their carefree imaginings about to become reality all too soon.

Liberated from the strict confines of her former life, Vera Mae wears suffrage colors with pride. Today, she's opted for a dark green skirt with a white blouse and a golden-yellow hat: the colors of the Women's Freedom League, for whom she regularly volunteers selling copies of *The Vote*. Tomorrow, she might wear the colors of the NUWSS. Always, she wears a thin silver wedding band on the appropriate finger of her left hand: a symbol of her commitment to Eulalie.

"Mamie! Mamie!" Flora drops down onto the blanket, her hands lightly clasped around the butterfly. "Look!" She opens up her palms to show her step-mother, but the butterfly seizes its chance for release and takes off from her thumb, fluttering away on the breeze. "Aww." She pouts, slumping against Vera Mae's lap.

"He's meant to be free, darling." Vera Mae straightens the ribbons in Flora's play-tousled hair. "No creature ought to be caged against its will." She checks the time on her wristwatch. "Now, we should get going. Mummy will be home shortly, and we want to be there to greet her, don't we?" She plants a quick kiss on Flora's head and brushes a little dirt off her summer dress, lamenting a grass stain she doubts Bennett will be able to get clean. "Come along."

She folds the picnic blanket into the basket, scoops it up in one arm and Flora in the other—something she could never have dreamed to do when corseted—and walks them back to the Grosvenor Square house, their arrival coinciding with the departure of Nell's doctor.

"Go on, love." Vera Mae sets Flora down and gives her a nudge toward the drawing room. "Go on in to your grandmother. I'm sure she could use some cheering up."

Once the bounding three-year-old is out of sight, Vera Mae helps the doctor with his hat and coat, inquiring as to the health of her ailing mother-in-law.

"How is she?"

"As good as can be expected." He gathers up his bag. "Plenty of rest is what she needs."

"I imagine she took that news exceedingly well." Vera Mae smirks.

"She hit me with her walking stick." The doctor rubs his arm. "Again."

Vera Mae sends him on his way with profuse apologies and the promise that Nell's cane will be removed from her prior to his next routine examination, then she joins Nell, Flora, and Bennett in the drawing room.

No longer strictly a lady's maid, Bennett sees directly to the needs of all the family as and when required, and is the only live-in domestic help. There's no butler, no footmen, and no housekeeper. Eulalie would've been quite happy to muddle along with no other staff at all, but

Vera Mae petitioned for a maid to do some charring three days a week, and a cook to prepare all the evening meals. Given Nell's failing health, and several burnt, utterly inedible roasts cooked by Vera Mae's inexperienced hands, the latter was an especially agreeable compromise.

"Stop fussing on me, girl." Nell relaxes on the sofa with Flora, resisting Bennett's efforts to cover her in a blanket. "I am not an invalid."

"You must let us do things for you, Mama." Vera Mae greets her with a peck on the cheek. "And stop abusing the doctor. The poor man's only doing his job."

At the sound of the front door, Flora dashes from the room. "Mummy!"

Vera Mae follows her into the hall, watching her collide with Eulalie the second she enters the house, both arms raised in the air, requesting to be picked up.

"Florrie!" Eulalie lifts her into an embrace. "Have you had fun with Mamie today?"

Flora nods, grinning. "Mamie tooked me to the park and I catched a butter-lie!" She clasps her hands together, demonstrating the technique.

"What a glorious adventure! You're such a lucky little girl." Eulalie kisses her. "Now, my sweet, why don't you pick out a game for us to play before dinner? I must have a quick bath and take care of Mamie." She returns Flora to the floor. "We shan't be long."

While Flora gallops back to Nell, Vera Mae takes her turn in Eulalie's loving arms and helps herself to a kiss.

"Going to 'take care' of Mamie, are you?"

"God, yes." Eulalie slips her hands onto Vera Mae's rump. "At least twice." She gives both buttocks a light spank.

"Best come upstairs with me, then." Vera Mae draws her to their bedroom, picking up a few of Flora's discarded toys along the way. "I don't know what I shall do with myself when Flora starts school." She sighs, depositing the toys on a sideboard. "I dread having to fill my days with knitting and sewing again. How frightfully mundane."

"It doesn't have to be that way." Eulalie doffs her jacket and tie, draping them over a red velvet chaise beneath Vera Mae's portrait. "We could always have another child."

"Don't tease." Vera Mae slips Eulalie's suspenders off her shoulders, then unbuttons her waistcoat and shirt. "You know this divine instrument of pleasure has its limitations." She drops one hand to Eulalie's crotch and grips the dildo hidden inside her trousers.

"And you know biology counts for very little when it comes to loving a babe." Eulalie divests herself of all clothing above her waist. "Why don't we adopt?"

"Are you quite serious?" Vera Mae unfastens her trousers and yanks them down.

"You're a wonderful mother, Vera." Eulalie works her French knickers over her hips and lets them drop to her ankles. "I want us to have more children. Surely you feel the same?"

Vera Mae offers no immediate answer. Instead, she unties the silk ribbon keeping the dildo secured to Eulalie's thigh and gives her a shove onto the foot of the bed, then kneels between her legs.

"Oh, good Lord." Eulalie moans in anticipation of what's coming. "I love watching you do this." She unpins Vera Mae's dark auburn mane and weaves her finger through it "No other woman has ever ... *ever* ..." She whimpers as Vera Mae drops a kiss on the tip of the priapus, then wraps her lips around it, sucking it completely into her mouth.

Though the business of fellating the glass cock began merely as an easy way to heat and lubricate the sturdy appendage when inspired to moments of impromptu passion outside the bedroom, it has since become an erotic delight in its own right. Were it real, Vera Mae would never dream of performing such a vulgar act, yet she finds nothing objectionable in this.

Once the thing's been suitably prepared for use, she rises from the carpeted floor, removes her knickers, hitches up her skirt, and pushes Eulalie onto her back, straddling her loins. "I need you inside me," she purrs, angling the phallus into her hungry sex, impaling herself inch by inch on the hot, wet glass.

In no hurry to reach the inevitable conclusion of their coupling, her movements are languid and precise. Entirely focused on her own pleasure, she rolls her hips, undulating on the rigid lance, both hands pressed to Eulalie's chest, her eyes closed and her head thrown back, moaning at the ceiling, bringing herself to the brink of orgasm again and again.

"Let me look at your charms." Eulalie attacks her blouse, camisole, and brassiere, stripping the garments away to release her weighty breasts. "So beautiful." She engulfs them in her hands. "So, so beautiful."

"I'm nearly there." Vera Mae groans urgently. "Finish me."

Commanded to do so, Eulalie grabs her hips, holds her in position, and fucks hard, thrusting fast and deep, the tapered head of the priapus kissing the gateway to her womb on every upstroke, making her wail through her climax. On the final plunge, she hilts herself and Vera Mae flops onto her chest, panting heavily.

"Sated?" Eulalie wraps her arms around Vera Mae's back.

"For the time being." Vera Mae giggles. "Till we catch our breath at least. And for my next pleasure, I should like to receive your oral attentions."

"Say it the way I like to hear it." Eulalie rolls onto her side, taking Vera Mae with her, their bodies still locked together. "Please."

Vera Mae colors up, bawdy language not yet coming naturally to her. "I want you to lick my cunt."

"That's better." Eulalie rewards her with a kiss. "I love you so much, Vera. I can't imagine my life without you." She strokes Vera Mae's pinkened cheeks. "After what happened with Percy, I feared you'd be strung up."

"It was self-defense." Vera Mae brings a hand to her neck, remembering how it felt to have his fingers clenched around her throat. "My skin bore the marks to prove as much."

"All the same." Eulalie nuzzles her nose. "You killed a man."

"I slew a monster," Vera Mae corrects her. "Just like Saint George." She hooks her leg over Eulalie's hip, anchoring herself and locking their bodies together. "Where were you headed that night? You never said, and we've never spoken of it."

"I was going to run." Eulalie cringes. "I went to the station and bought a ticket, but when my train came ... I didn't get on it. I couldn't. I came back to face him."

"A train to where?" Vera Mae probes, grinding against her.

"Henfield, Sussex." Eulalie reciprocates every wiggle of her bum. "A suffragette called Elizabeth Robins has a farmhouse near there. She uses it as a retreat for other suffragettes recovering from hunger strike, or for those on the run from the police. I planned to send word to my mother and have her meet me there with Flora."

"Elizabeth Robins ... I know her." The name rings a bell in Vera Mae's memory banks. "She's an actress, yes? She wrote a suffrage play, *Votes for Women!* It was produced at the Royal Court Theatre some years ago. I was twenty-four, not yet married, and had to steal away from my father's house in Belgrave Square to see it. I shall never forget the thrill of it all."

"I saw it, too." Eulalie smiles. "Shortly before I married. I was nineteen." She rolls on top of Vera Mae, keeping the dildo embedded. "Imagine if we were there at the same time. Imagine if we'd met all those years ago. We could've eloped."

"But then we wouldn't have Flora." Vera Mae wraps her legs around Eulalie's lower back, heels to bum, mewling as Eulalie moves inside her. "And the answer's yes, by the way." She buries her fingers in Eulalie's tousled hair and pulls her into a kiss. "Let's adopt."

The Fight for the Right to Vote

In the lead up to the First World War, more than 1,000 British suffragettes were imprisoned for acts of violence committed while lobbying for women's rights. Primarily, the right to vote.

The violence escalated after the first conciliation bill was shot down by Prime Minister Asquith in 1910—an act which led directly to Black Friday. A second conciliation bill was dropped in 1911, and a third defeated by parliamentary vote in 1912.

In 1918, the right to vote was granted to some women over the age of thirty: those who were property owners, those who were members of—or married to members of—the Local Government Register, and those who were university graduates voting in a university constituency.

In 1928, women in the UK were finally granted the right to vote on the same terms as men.

About the Author

Keira Michelle Telford is an award-winning author with a love for the gruesome, the macabre, and the downright filthy. She writes historical and contemporary erotic sapphic romance, and other sapphic fiction.

Erotic Lesbian Romance
Cadence of My Heart
The Housemistress

Historical Lesbian Romance
The Ruin of Us
Quicunque Vult

Short Stories
Hoar & Rime
Evonnia & the Maiden
Falling Hard

Futanari
All the Devils (short story)
Come, My Pet

Website: www.keiramichelle.com
Twitter: @km_telford
Facebook: www.facebook.com/keiramichelletelford
Goodreads: www.goodreads.com/keiramichelle
Amazon: www.amazon.com/author/keiramichelle